A Death of Innocence

Richard A. Hackett Jr.

A Death of Innocence

For more information about the author and other novels or books he has written, please visit the authors website at:

www.rhackettjr.com

Excluding those mentioned in the Bible, the additional characters and events in this book are fictional, and any resemblance to actual persons or events is coincidental.

ISBN-13: 9798327589353
Imprint: Independently published

Copyright © 2024 by Richard A Hackett Jr.

All rights reserved. No part of this book may be reproduced or transmitted in any form or by any means, electronic or mechanical, including photocopying and recording, or by any informational storage or retrieval system, without permission in writing from the author/publisher.

Acknowledgements

To the many Nathan's in my Christian walk who always chose to protect the flock and fellowship of believers from those in positions of authority who would abuse it. Who cared more about pleasing God than pleasing men, often suffering greater persecution and abuse by those same leaders than what the world we strove to be separated from ever did.

Please know that you are a member of a long list of courageous men and women who by taking a stand against evil, may have endured personal slander, character assassinations, malignment, and even been discarded by the same fellowship you tried to protect. Rest assured, God is pleased with your efforts as a Watchman for his people (Ezekiel 33:1-9) and a protector of His honor and will award your courage in this life or the next.

About A Death of Innocence

From everyone who has been given much, much will be demanded; and from the one who has been entrusted with much, much more will be asked.
Luke 12:48

Since the beginning of creation God has given us the incredible gift of *free will*. A gift that allows us to make choices, and then act on those choices, either for the glory of God or for our own glory. The challenge and danger of such an incredible gift is that the greater the position and power one has over others, the greater the opportunity for someone to abuse that gift for selfish gain.

David's life is an incredible example of *free will* being lived out, for both good and evil in life and leadership. Unfortunately, the two chapters in 2 Samuel 11-12 would prove to be one of the greatest and most pivotal *free will* leadership failures for David. A series of selfish choices and far-reaching consequences that would not only shatter the innocence and lives of those caught up in them, but the innocence of his own heart and reputation as a man after God's own heart. It was *a death of innocence* that would forever tarnish and weaken his trust as a leader of a nation, and the trust needed as a father, husband, and a friend.

Our nature can be to quickly read through a story in the Bible and just gather a list of the facts from it (the 'what' of the story). However, God included each of these incredible stories (big or small) for a reason. He wants us to slow down and search for the reason behind the story (the 'why' of the story) and to discover and understand the hearts of the characters of the people within them. Only then can we discover the incredible learning opportunities hidden within it and how they apply to our own lives. *This book was written for that purpose.*

Richard Hackett Jr.

Chapter 1
A Battle of the Heart
(David)

What have I done? David thought to himself as he stared out over the city of Jerusalem from the 3rd floor balcony attached to his palace room. Even though it was extremely late in the evening, the full moon and clear skies revealed the city he loved so dearly spread out below him, shrouded in an eerie hue of black and white. The vibrant spring colors that could normally be seen in the daylight were now gone, leaving only dark shadows and a deep silence. His heart felt the same, void of color and majesty. As he surveyed the city, his eyes tried to avoid the area, but the pain in his chest kept drawing them back to the rooftop below that had started it all.

He could still smell her perfume on his clothes and hands, a combination of many spices and fragrances, the most dominant one being cinnamon. In the moment of passion, he had loved the smell of the cinnamon in her hair and on her skin, but now, in the aftermath of his sin, he hated the smell that seemed to have seeped into his very soul.

Two days prior, she was the most beautiful women he had ever seen as he watched her bathing in the sunlight as he allowed his inner passion to grow with each moment. He knew in his heart of hearts that he should have turned away, even reached out with an invitation to one of his wives to appease the passion, but instead he allowed his eyes to take in her full beauty.

Instead of turning away, he had even stepped into the shadows of a nearby overhang to help conceal his presence, allowing him to watch her until she had completed her task. The longer he stood there, the more he burned inside for her, a burning that had driven out all reason and common sense. He had at first wrestled with his decision to embrace the sinful lust of the moment, but as time passed, he had somehow justified it and gave into it fully. As she was leaving her roof, David saw her pause and glance toward the only building in the city high enough that could infringe upon her privacy. It was as if she looked right at him. *Had she seen him,* he wondered? *Perhaps she wanted him to see her?* He reasoned. All he could remember now was the series of selfish decisions and horrible choices that followed. All of which he could have stopped at any moment but was unwilling to. Even now, although the event had passed, he could remember all the selfish thoughts and feelings that had driven him forward.

Who was she? David had wondered. The ongoing war with the Ammonites and the duties of leading the armies of Israel against them, rarely allowed him to spend time in Jerusalem, let alone know who lived near the palace. Thus, he had no idea who the beautiful woman was, so he sent someone to inquire.

"She is Bathsheba, the daughter of Eliam and the wife of Uriah the Hittite." The man he had sent to inquire reported.[1]

His heart at first sank at the news. Uriah was one of his best warriors and a loyal and trusted leader. *When had Uriah married and why had he not been invited to the wedding?* David wondered. However, despite learning she was married, the fire inside was not quenched by the report, but grew in strength and purpose. Instead of wrestling with the lustful fire, he embraced it.

A Hittite warrior as great as Uriah would have many wives and Bathsheba was probably just one of his many concubines, David remembered reasoning selfishly. Besides, Uriah had not only pledged his loyalty to David when becoming one of his mighty men, he had demonstrated it in battle more times than David could remember. Ignoring the internal moral warnings and consequences of such thoughts, he finally concluded and reasoned that the Hittites were one of the conquered peoples and therefore subject to his Kingdom and under his authority.

As he had done so many times before in his life to defeat his enemies, he began to develop the most clever and effective strategy that would defeat her will and achieve his desires. However, Bathsheba was not his enemy, but the wife of a fellow soldier and friend.

Ignoring the ongoing warnings whispering from his heart, he had sent a series of messages to Bathsheba in hopes he would gradually win her confidence and trust. The initial message innocently praised her husband's prowess in battle and his complete loyalty to David as his King. The second message he had sent alluded to the deep bond and loyalty that exists between soldiers and their families, a mindset that he hoped Bathsheba would fully embrace. The final message he had sent, simply stated "The King invites you and a personal chaperone to the palace this evening for dinner." The messenger returned with a short message from Bathsheba thanking the King and confirming the dinner invitation. Although in his mind his stated goal that the 'dinner invitation' would be just that, he knew in his heart he was determined to quench the consuming fire burning within him.

When Bathsheba arrived, David was once again stunned by her beauty. He could see that she had prepared herself to meet the king and was dressed elegantly, yet modestly. Although her chaperone was included in the initial introductions and discussions before dinner, when the food was ready, David made it subtly clear to Bathsheba that her chaperone was not included in the dinner portion of the evening. David knew that leaving a married woman alone with another man was not proper procedure, so he pretended to ignore the moment of silent awkwardness that followed. Eventually Bathsheba dismissed her handmaiden with a nod of her head and slight motion of her hand. The chaperone paused briefly, as if to argue the command, but then bowed to the king and left the two alone.

David could not remember all the discussion, only that he had a carefully thought-out, step-by-step strategy that he hoped would lead to achieving his goal. He spent the early part of the evening meal making toasts that praised the loyalty of Bathsheba's husband Uriah to David, each toast encouraged Bathsheba to consume more and more wine in the process. He waited patiently until he saw that the wine was beginning to have its effect on her. As the meal was winding down, he shifted his praise to Bathsheba's beauty. Although she would blush at the compliments, he could see that she also relished the attention and thanked him.

He could still remember the moment when his inner being was shouting at him to *stop this madness*, but he quickly silenced it and stumbled forward like a lamb to the slaughter. Instead of avoiding the growing opportunity the wine was creating within Bathsheba, he responded like a general seeing the opportunity on the battlefield and attacked her weakest defenses.

He could still remember the bitter taste of deceit and manipulation as he explained how he understood and empathized with how difficult it must be for the wife of a soldier who has been away for so long. He remembered her nodding and smiling sadly. Seeing her defenses weakening, he asked if her loyalty to her King was as devout as that of her husband. David remembered the moment of silence as Bathsheba wrestled with the meaning of the question and the consequences of her response. Whether it was the wine, the loneliness, her unfounded trust in him, the manipulative pressure of his position as king, or all of them combined, she eventually nodded and looked down at her empty plate.

A falling star in the dark night sky brought him back to the reality of the present. *How appropriate* he thought as he shook his head and he tried to forget what followed. What took days of deceitful planning and preparation to create was over in a moment of passion and lust. He had gone from king to adulterer, protector to predator, trusted friend to betrayer, and from a man after God's own heart to one after his own.

His moment of self-pity was interrupted as he remembered how he pretended to be asleep as he watched Bathsheba slowly slide out of his bed to dress and prepare to leave. It was over, and he could see the shame and hurt on her face. She was now an adulteress. There were no words to share that could make it right, no way to reverse time to change what had just happened. He pretended to be awakened by her departure and stopped her from leaving through the main door. He motioned to a different door than the one she had come in through. "Let's keep this secret between us," he had said, and she seemed to wrestle with the suggestion. "There are too many people that could be hurt, even the very kingdom of Israel, if this were to be known." David's voice sounded more like a command than a request with the second statement, but he tried to conceal it by smiling as he touched her face in a false romantic gesture. She nodded and returned a faint, but disappointed smile before stepping through the door that he knew would lead her through an empty hallway ending near the palace entrance.

As he stood looking over the colorless city from his balcony, he continued to wrestle with guilt and shame. He even contemplated the idea of speaking to Nathan about the sin he had just committed, even knew he should. However, his mind was suddenly filled with a flood of all the terrible consequences such an approach would generate. The visions of humiliation, the loss of respect, and the guilt he would feel the next time he saw his wives, or as he walked through the streets, or at the head of his army. He felt as if the multitude of fears flowing through his head were drowning him.

What would Uriah do should he find out? Would he seek vengeance? Deep down David was confident that he would. Would others try to take his throne in his moment of weakness? He knew that Joab and his brother were always looking for an opportunity to take control. He shook his head at the thought. No one could know, it would be a secret that only Bathsheba and he would carry the rest of their lives.

He took a deep breath and exhaled as he looked out over the city again. He was the king and the people looked up to him. Although what he had done was not right, he decided that protecting the kingdom and its leaders was far more important than any sins committed by them. Although tainted, he felt he had earned that right.

As if looking for confirmation, his mind raced back through time as he relived the challenges he faced and the victories he had achieved in his life. Although anointed king, he was forced to suffer the abuse of Saul. He had lost his wife, his best friend, was forced to live in caves, endured hardship and starvation, and yet he waited patiently for God to enthrone him. Once he became king, he drove out invaders, defeated great armies, won impossible battles, and expanded the borders of Israel to her near prophesied boundaries. He was weary of war and simply needed companionship. He glanced again at the city before him and the kingdom he now ruled. Then he suddenly remembered that this was the same inner dialog that had brought him to the rooftop where he witnessed Bathsheba's bath. *It was all God's will*, he finally reasoned.

David jumped at the sudden knock on his door. A knock that broke the silence and scattered his thoughts. As he opened it, a servant was standing nervously before him with a lantern.

"My King, Nathan the prophet is at the palace entrance and asking if you are well." The servant stated. David at first was shocked by the arrival of Nathan and his asking such a question at this late hour.

"Tell him that the King says that all is well, and he will meet with him in the morning when he wakes." David replied almost angrily, and the servant nodded and headed back down the hallway. As David shut the door, he tried to think of the timeline from when Bathsheba had left and Nathan's arrival. He knew that there was not enough time for her to make it to the temple to confess their sin even if she had run. He exhaled and relaxed knowing that no one could have known about what had happened.

Chapter 2
Dreams & Visions
(Nathan)

Nathan stood in the entryway of the palace, nervously waiting for word from King David. Nathan had awoken from a dream where he had seen David in great danger as he stood at a crossroads contemplating which direction to go. Somehow Nathan knew that one path led to victory and the other to defeat at the hands of an enemy of God. The wrong choice would lead to much suffering for not only him, but for the nation of Israel. He had tried to yell a warning to him, but he could not speak. He tried to run to him to point him in the right direction, but his legs would not move. All he could do was watch his king struggle with the decision before him. At first it looked as if he would choose wisely, but at the last minute he changed direction. Nathan suddenly woke from his dream and his heart was beating fast and his body covered in sweat.

Although it was late, almost morning, he immediately got dressed and ran to the palace, wondering if the dream was from God or from a fever. He had learned to assume everything was a message from God, even though they often did not turn out to be. As he ran to the palace, there were no trumpets calling men to war nor were fires being lit in preparation. In fact, there was no activity at all, except for an older man relieving himself in an alley and two women with their cloaks and hoods pulled tightly around their faces hurrying down the street, nervously holding each other's hand. As his path was about to cross theirs, he wondered what event created a need for them to be out so late in the evening. He contemplated stopping to ask about their wellbeing or if they had heard of any concerning news, but his concern for the king overruled it. Unable to see their faces, he nodded and smiled briefly as they passed by.

With the palace gate now in sight, he slowed his pace and tried to catch his breath before approaching the guards. It was at that moment that the smell of a rare spice carried by the wind caught his attention. At first Nathan could not remember the fragrance, for such spices were rare in Jerusalem, but then it came to him. It was cinnamon.

Nathan was once again relieved to see the palace guards at their entry gate posts and apparently unaware of any dangers. As Nathan approached, they were at first tense and prepared as they lowered their spears at his sight, but then returned to their normal stance as they recognized him and nervously nodded. Nathan found that people were often nervous around prophets, fearing they could somehow read their minds and know all their secrets, which he could not. A series of loud taps were generated by one of the guards as he struck the end of his spear onto the rock flooring. Moments later, a smaller passage door was opened for Nathan to enter. Once through the doorway, he was greeted by a nervous and disheveled servant, obviously caught unprepared for a visit this late in the evening and was led into the palace's great room.

"My lord, how may I be of service to you?" he asked Nathan. Nathan tried to think of how he was going to explain his concern for the king without revealing his dream to everyone.

"Is the king well?" was all he said in reply. The servant seemed confused but knowing the often peculiar and strange ways of prophets and holy men, he knew it was a serious question.

"Yes... I mean he's sleeping at this late hour." He answered nervously.

"Can you verify his health for me?" Nathan replied without breaking eye contact to make sure he knew he was serious about the request, knowing that servants did not like disturbing their masters at such late hours. To avoid the kings wrath, such requests would have to be of a profoundly serious matter or from someone of high rank. After a brief pause, the servant nodded.

"Wait here and I will wake the king on your behalf," he said with a slight emphasis on 'your' and then adjusted his cloak and hair as he excused himself.

As Nathan waited, he glanced at the multitude of items hanging on the walls, sitting on the floor, or laying on various tables spread around the palace great room. There were bronze shields, swords, goblets, and even crowns of gold and silver. Most of them were items taken from vanquished enemies; others were gifts to the king. God had truly blessed his people and had raised an incredible leader to guide them. David was so unlike any man Nathan had ever known. He had a single-minded passion and love for God and a deep love and humility toward others. As a result of that love, few feared his leadership, unless it was against him in battle, but all respected him and desired to imitate the special relationship he had with God, a relationship that was pure, simple, and filled with faith. His humility as a leader was also infectious and it drew many people to him. There were those that viewed such humility as weakness, but they could not deny that God was with him in all that he did.

Nathan took a deep breath and smiled as he walked around the dimly lit room. He felt so honored and blessed to be alive at this time in Israel's history. The Promised Land that so many prophets had spoken of was now nearly secured and their enemies either in flight or vanquished. Despite all the wars and inner tribal fighting the land was flourishing and the people were happy and they loved their King. Their last enemies, the Ammonites, were now hiding behind their fortress walls surrounded by the army of Israel. Life was good, and it seemed that peace for the people of Israel was finally within reach.

The sound of footsteps halted Nathan's thoughts as he turned to see the servant approaching him.

The King said to tell you "All is well, and he will meet with you in the morning when he wakes," the servant finished with a slightly frustrated look on his face. "Is there anything else you need?" He asked.

Nathan at first hesitated, sorting through his dream as if there were some clues or meaning he had missed. To learn that he was sleeping and well put to rest his greatest concern. Nathan finally shook his head. "No. Thank you for humoring my request," he said and then turned to leave. "Sleep well," he said as he left.

Nathan's walk home from the palace was far less stressful and urgent than his walk to it had been. He took the time to take in the majesty and immenseness of the stars, and moon, and to pray and give thanks to the Lord. He prayed for David's health and safety, for the soldiers fighting Israel's enemies, for the people caught between the battles and wars who seemed to suffer the most during such times.

David's kingship was a result of the people's desire to imitate the other kingdoms around them[1]. God had made it clear to the people the dangers and consequences of turning away from a total reliance and trust in Him, relying instead in a man to lead them. Despite the warning, the people wanted a king. God allowed it to begin with Saul, and although tall and handsome, the people witnessed the consequences of pursuing such a faithless leadership style. However, like with all things, God is always looking out for his people and had put plans in motion for an earthly king to lead them even before Saul's reign was over. A king after God's own heart, not after his own. That "heart for God" was what set David apart from the faithless approach to leadership that Saul took, where fear, insecurity and pride ruled.

Nathan took one more glance at the stars and smiled before heading back into the temple. Instead of returning to his bed, he decided he would read and pray until morning, where he would then enjoy the majesty and beauty of the sunrise.

1 - (1 Samuel 8:1-22)

Chapter 3
Trust & Loyalty
(Uriah)

Uriah watched as the water dripped from his head and beard, down into the stream below him. The ripples slowly faded as the drops slowed and his face came into view within the reflection of the water. He smiled at how refreshing the water felt after a challenging training session with his men. Flipping his hair back and running his fingers through it to help keep it in place, he walked over and sat against a rock and watched his men following his lead. Some were laughing and jostling with each other as they washed their heads in the cool water of the stream, others were clearly exhausted and more interested in recovering than cooling down or participating in any added revelry.

He was proud of his men and would die for them if needed. Although he was a Hittite, he had won the respect and loyalty of these men by leading from the front lines of battle, not from the safety behind the lines. They also saw his sworn loyalty to King David and to the people of Israel. As his first leadership assignment, Uriah and his men had been viewed by many as a group of misfits, but after the intensive and ongoing training style he implemented from his Hittite upbringing, they had become one of the fiercest and most effective fighting units in the army. He knew it, they knew it, and everyone else knew it.

A roar of laughter arose as one of the men had used his helmet to pour the cold water over the head and down the neck of an unsuspecting member who had been too tired to join them at the stream.

"For being so tired, he sure moves fast!" one of the men watching chimed in as the victim had angrily jumped to his feet, unsuccessfully trying to catch his attacker.

"Not fast enough," his attacker added quickly moving beyond the man's wrath. Uriah smiled as he saw the victim's initially shocked and angry face relax and his revengeful pursuit cease. The man took a deep breath and instead enjoyed the sensation of the cool water dripping down his back and out the bottom of his tunic.

"Thank you. You saved me from wasting my energy on doing that myself," he finally said, trying to somehow turn the momentary defeat into a victory. This of course only brought more humorous chiding from the other soldiers.

Uriah loved his men as only fellow soldiers who had trained and fought side by side could. Trained as a soldier during the fading glory of the Hittite kingdom, he had heard of David's victories against their enemies while serving in the southern defenses. While the Hittite king was making treaties with his enemies instead of vanquishing them as they had before, David was laying claim to the area Uriah's former god had promised his people. Although the stories of David's God were well known among the kingdoms surrounding Israel, it was David's leadership and courage in battle that had drawn Uriah to pledge his sword to him, however his love and faith in David's God came after. It was Uriah's courage and skill in the ongoing battles with the Philistines that had won him favor in the eyes of King David. Since then, even though Uriah was a Hittite, David had promoted him into one of the highest leadership positions in the Israelite army.

Uriah loved David, not only as a king, but as a distant and desired friend, a man of character and wisdom. The only person on this earth that he loved more was his wife Bathsheba. He took a deep breath and smiled at the thought of her. He longed to hold her in his arms, to caress her face and kiss her lips. It was these longings and the thought that she was safely protected behind the walls of Jerusalem, and out of the reach of any enemy, that kept his focus on serving. He longed for the day when this last war with the Ammonites was over, and he could return to her. They wanted to have many babies and grow old together, but until then he would give his heart to his king and to this war. Remembering that his king was in Jerusalem made him feel more at peace that his wife was safe.

With the rest and refreshment time over, Uriah stood again and addressed his men with a heavy Hittite accent. "We move as one, we fight as one, we win as one, and if it is God's will, we die as one for our God and our King's glory, not our own. As the prophets have written, we are to love God with all our heart, mind, soul and strength and to love each other as ourselves," He stated, remembering the words he had learned and practiced from the Torah. His men nodded as they gathered around him.

"As one!" They began to shout and cheer repeatedly with smiles and greater determination. The sound grew louder with each repeating of the chant, and it filled the immediate area and even carried to the other members of the Israelite army.

"As one!" Uriah shouted back with his sword arm raised and then as he slowly lowered, the cheers and shouts faded until once again only silence remained. "The Philistine fortress is well defended and gaining their walls will be difficult without a good plan and the courage needed to take them. But remember, when these walls fall and the completion of our promised homeland is fulfilled, we can then return to our families and homes. We are perhaps but a single battle away from these dreams and longings, but only if our faith and resolve remain true." Uriah shouted so that all could hear and walked amongst his men, stopping to clasp hands and give pats on the shoulders.

"Although I am not born an Israelite, you have welcomed me into your nation and introduced me to your God Yahweh, whom I have embraced, and your king, whom I am honored to follow. As a Hittite, I am a warrior by nature and training, and I have much to learn of your God. However, I have seen enough of your king to know that he is a man of honor and courage. His steadfast love and obedience to God is one that I desire to imitate as I learn more. Although I have learned to speak your awkward and frustrating language," he paused and smiled as his men responded with smiles and laughter, "unfortunately, I cannot read your strange letters and have difficulty making long speeches. So, despite my slow progression and low intelligence." Uriah paused and looked around and smiled, "yes, I know that is what you are thinking," his men laughed in response and nodded. "Let us continue to honor and fulfill our agreement with each other. I will teach you how to wage war in battle, and you will teach me how to better honor and serve your God in heart, mind, soul and spirit," he said, and they nodded proudly in response.

"Dathan, would you lead these men back to camp, so they don't get lost," Uriah ordered one of his leaders, with a smile, who nodded in return. At first, Dathan pointed the men toward the wrong direction and then smiled toward Uriah and turned toward camp.

Uriah shook his head. "The blind leading the blind, what hope have we?" he called out and the men and Dathan smiled.

"We have you!" one of the men shouted and others nodded in agreement as they marched away. Those three words carried a great deal of weight for Uriah. Where he led these men they would follow, whether the direction he led them was good or bad. Trust and loyalty were invaluable, but often truth and honesty being spoken at the right time was far more valuable.

Chapter 4
Understanding power
(Joab)

For the hundredth time, Joab Zeruiah surveyed the distant walls of the Ammonite city of Rabbah from the nearby hilltop. His army had surrounded the city and laid siege to it hoping this would be the last battle against this adversary. *His army*, he thought. That statement would probably not be completely accurate if you were to ask the people of Israel, or even those assembled in this army. However, he was officially in charge of it until David returned.

He thought of the many battles that had been fought over the past years to secure the land promised by God to the nation of Israel. There seemed to be an endless list of nearby adversary nations all trying to destroy God's people. Although he despised them all, he was hard pressed to decide which of them he reviled the most. After a moment of reflection, two stood out to him, it would either be the Ammonites or the Philistines. For decades, these two nations[1] had been far more than a thorn in Israel's side[2], they had been the greatest threat to their very existence as a people. In addition to their already vast numbers, fortresses and superior weaponry, they often would use their great wealth to hire additional mercenaries and recruit allies from the surrounding territories to bolster their numbers and chances of victory. Israel had none.

Although the idea of living together in peace had been extended to them many times, their only interest was to either subjugate or destroy the people of Israel. Joab remembered the endless numbers of chariots brought to battle against them, a weapon that was effective in the plains, but not as lethal in the hill country. He remembered the many opportunities his army had looting their enemy's bodies after a battle, marveling at all their protective armor and superior weapons. They even had giants[3] leading their armies into battle, the very offspring of the Nephilim mentioned in the Torah[4]. Yet each of these enemies had all fallen to Israel's fewer numbers and basic weaponry, not by might and expertise, but by the faith in, and the guidance and power of the God of Israel.

Joab knew it was Saul who had defeated the Amalekites, and he and his son Jonathan had struck the first blow against the Philistines in Beth Aven, but those victories had only come when God was with them. When Saul was rejected by God, there were few victories and far more defeats at the hands of these enemies. Even when David, God's anointed, stepped out of obscurity and struck down Goliath and drove back the Philistines, it was a dark time for Israel while Saul remained King. Even when David was in exile, he became the target of Saul's rage and jealousy that would turn the tribes of Israel against each other. Without God's blessings, that jealousy would lead not only to Saul's death at the hands of the Philistines, but the death of his son Jonathan as well. It also cost the life of Joab's brother Asahel, leaving only his brother Abishai and him as the surviving members of the Zeruiah family.

Although Joab knew that Jonathan was a good man and a brave warrior, he also knew David and Jonathan were close. So close that Jonathan would have eventually been an obstacle to his own leadership and relationship with David. Although Jonathan's death was unfortunate, Joab was happy he no longer had to consider him a threat.

David, with Joab's help, ultimately unified the people under one King and defeated the Philistines. Even so, the taste of victory and peace was short lived, as another adversary stepped forward, the Ammonites. Just as they were victorious over the Philistines with God's intervention and David and Joab's leadership, one by one, they defeated the Ammonite's repeated attempts to destroy them. Once again, Joab and his brother Abishai were there with David at every battle and victory.

Joab had come to learn that his skills and talents were not in leading a nation or people, but in battle and power. Where he saw black and white with each decision, David could somehow see all the colors and the bigger picture and purpose each decision required. Oddly, he not only understood Saul's jealousy of David after he defeated Goliath, but he could also relate to it. He had not only been there at each victory, but he often was the commander of those victories, or played a decisive role in them, yet David always received the glory and credit for them.

Strange how that one blow that brought down Goliath had not only turned the destiny of the nation of Israel, but it also firmly established David's name among the people, and they were drawn to him. Like many of Saul's decisions, right or wrong, Joab felt it was his obligation and purpose to make the hard decisions in the moment, decisions that would not only achieve victory, but the ones that David was often too afraid to make himself. He made those decisions to protect David, the people, and often even his own position. As a result of those decisions, people feared him, yet they loved David. If that was the role he would need to play to maintain his power and position, then so be it.

As he surveyed the area again, he realized what was missing. "Where is Uriah and his men?" he asked his brother Abishai, who was always by his side.

"I was told he took them to the river for refreshment and training," Abishai replied and then smiled as he waited for his brother's response. Joab shook his head and grimaced at what had become a common practice of Uriah. Joab felt disrespected and knew that if Uriah and his men had not proven to be so valuable and effective in battle, he would have Uriah's head for such disregard of his leadership and direct orders.

"Does he remind you of anyone?" his brother asked and then chuckled. Joab knew to whom he was referring and he did not like it when his brother reminded him of his past. Joab knew that of all the men in his army, Uriah would be David's next choice to take his position should something unplanned occur to him or his brother. "No leader or group works harder for you than Uriah and his men. They have been the sharpest and deadliest force in your army, and you know it," Abishai counseled him. "Brother, they've earned it, so give them their time of refreshment at the river," Abishai said and patted his brother on the shoulder. "Who knows, maybe it will inspire others to higher paths of glory."

Joab thought about his brother's perspective and suggestion, but then shook his head. "No, such disobedience to my direct commands would spread like yeast through the army." He replied angrily.

Abishai shook his head and was surprised by Joab's response. "Brother, you gave no orders to Uriah or any other leader that they could not take their men to the river."

"No, but out of respect for me he should have asked for permission. He would have never done that if David were here," Joab replied sharply. Although he knew his brother was right, he was growing more upset with each response.

Abishai shook his head and turned to leave, "You're right, if David was here, he would not have cared. Perhaps he would have even recommended it to them." Abishai paused as he was walking away, "Perhaps you should spend less time worrying that you are living in David's shadow and instead learn from it and enjoy the shade it provides you and the men," he stated and then walked away.

The words cut Joab deeply, words that only a brother would know how to use with maximum effect, yet at the same time knowing it would not lead to his head being removed from his body. Joab shook with anger. *Even my brother views David as a better leader than I*, he thought and turned back toward the walls of Rabbah and the challenge before him.

[1] Judges 14:3
[2] 1 Samuel 13:19-20
[3] Numbers 13:33
[4] 1 Samuel 17:4-7

Chapter 5
Consequence of sin
(David)

As the weeks passed, David felt more and more confident that Bathsheba had honored his request and had not revealed their unfortunate encounter to anyone else. Although he regretted his actions, he could not help replaying the evening over and over in his head. Initially his thoughts focused on the 'what ifs' if someone were to find out. However, as time passed and the possibilities of it being discovered faded, his thoughts shifted more towards replaying the more carnal and pleasurable aspects of the act.

At first it was the feeling of guilt that filled his heart with each thought, but as time passed and he relived each new remembrance of the event, the feeling of guilt was gradually and strangely replaced with a sense of conquest or victory. It was not a feeling of a warrior's victory, but something far less noble. The best description he could find for it was a victory in battle not won by skill or ability, but by luck, trickery or deception; a hollow victory, the methods of which one would prefer would never come to light, but a victory nonetheless.

Although his lustful thoughts of Bathsheba persisted, David's conviction was that no matter what situation presented itself, he would take the righteous path from here forward. Although he did not reveal or confess what he had done to Nathan the prophet, he did spend more time thereafter listening to and learning from him and the insights of God that he shared. He felt that God was slowly removing the burden of guilt from his heart. In appreciation, he put more time and energy into meeting the needs of the orphans and widows of the soldiers that had been lost in battle within his army. Although he considered reaching out to Bathsheba and apologizing for his actions, he felt it was best to not bring the moment up again and that time would heal all.

As he prepared for the day's events, during which all the day's events were either being laid out in front of him for his review and signature or explained in detail by his assistants, a messenger stepped into the room. David could sense the urgency of the messenger's desire to share his news, so he held up a hand, halting the most current presentation, and the assistants stepped back from the table. As the messenger came forward, he spoke quietly and clearly to David explaining that a female messenger named Talia was requesting a private audience with him. Not recognizing the name, David seemed confused by the request until the messenger said she was from Uriah's household.

At first David was puzzled as to what the need might be. If Bathsheba had reported what happened to Nathan, it would not have been someone from her household that would be asking for a meeting. If she had said something to Uriah, then he knew it would be Uriah at his door with sword in hand. His heart jumped at the next thought that crossed his mind, *she must want to meet again*. Would he be willing to entertain such a request and risk reigniting that flame within him? Although his mind quietly said *no*, his heart screamed *yes*. He nodded to the messenger and asked that she be sent in. As was the typical response, the room cleared for their private conversation. *How would she ask?* he wondered as he waited for the assistants to leave and the messenger to arrive. Probably with an innocent inquiry or invitation to dinner in appreciation for his leadership. Perhaps an honest sharing of her heart and love for him? His heart was beating faster in anticipation of the various opportunities that awaited him. Then the door opened, and the messenger entered the room and moments later the door was closed behind her, and a silence filled the room. She glanced around the room as if making sure they were alone.

At first David did not recognize the stern-faced women standing before him, then as the lustful anticipation faded, he remembered her. She was Bathsheba's escort the night of their encounter. He remembered how concerned and unhappy she was when Bathsheba had dismissed her from her protective duties that night. David knew she had waited loyally outside and was there to escort her home when the evening was over, knowing exactly what must have happened and how she had failed her employer. David tried to read her face as the awkward silence persisted, but there was nothing he could gather. David was confident that she would not be happy whether she was delivering an invitation to meet, or any other request. Except perhaps his head on a platter.

"Hello Talia, how can I be of assistance to your household?" David asked and waited for her response. She did not speak, but instead reached into her sleeve to retrieve something hidden there. At first, he prepared to defend himself from the thrust of a dagger or short sword, but then felt confident that his men had searched her for such dangers. It was not until the small leather tube became visible that he realized it was a written message being delivered. She then took two steps and set it on the edge of his desk without speaking.

Once again, David tried to read her expression again, but her face was as cold as the last time. He reached across the table and picked up the leather tube. There were no letters or markings on the leather tube, probably to avoid revealing the owner of the message should it fall into someone else's hands. David carefully broke the wax seal and slid the small piece of paper out of the tube. As he carefully unrolled the scroll, his heart sank as he read the Hebrew words.

"I am with child."

He glanced at the messenger and although her expression had not changed, the anger in her eyes burned through him.

"Please send my congratulations to…" David tried to reply cordially before she cut him off sharply.

"There has been no one else. With Uriah away loyally fighting your foes, you are the only one that has been with her in the past 4 months." She said coldly, making it clear that David is the only one who could be responsible.

His mind raced in panic as he searched for the right words to use. Of all the responses he had prepared and planned to use should any of the various possibilities of discovery happened, he had never thought of one for this situation. She was carrying his child and there was no way to hide it from Uriah, let alone the rest of the world around her. She would be put to death when others found out of her adultery, perhaps by Uriah himself. Contrary to his hope that the tragic event would slowly fade away and be forgotten, the evidence of his guilt, and the ultimate revealing of it, had been growing inside of Bathsheba the whole time. David suddenly realized that contrary to his belief, God had not shielded him from the consequences of his sin.

His mind raced, trying to find a way to make things right again, but no matter which path his mind took him down, he could find no escape. Then his mind found the opening to a very dark path, and he let his mind explore it. *Would she be willing to give up her life and the life of the child to protect their secret?* He has repeatedly risked his life for the people of Israel, would it be too much to ask for her to do the same in return? At first David leaned into the thought and the possibilities of such a noble path for her. However, whether it was the Spirit of God or just a moment of moral clarity warning him from such a path, he finally turned away from it. Before he realized he was even speaking, he gave his answer.

"Tell her that I'm sure we can find a way to resolve this problem," then pausing briefly he realized the gravity of this moment for Bathsheba and his response to the news. He tried to fully grasp what Bathsheba and her servant must be thinking and then continued. "Tell her I'm sorry and I know this is my fault, but I ask her to be patient." David said softly and as he allowed his body to fall against the back of his chair.

At David's initial response, Talia's face finally revealed what her eyes had hidden, and she even let her head shake in disagreement. Then it changed when he took ownership of the situation and what he had done to put her in it. Although she was still angry, she nodded in relief at his response. Did she really think he would have allowed her to lose her life as if she were nothing to him? Then he remembered the dark path that had crossed his mind and how easily he could have gone down it. It shocked him to think that was the path she had expected him to take.

"Tell her I am so sorry and that I will do everything I can as king to make this right," David finally said after a long silence. She recognized her dismissal and bowed and then turned, opened the door and walked out. David motioned to his assistant to shut the door behind her.

He sat in silence as all the guilt, fear and shame came flooding back into his thoughts. After a long period of confusion, he stood and walked to the window that overlooked the city. "Why God have you added to my shame? Have I not suffered enough for your name and glory? I've been chased by a mad king whom you anointed, I've suffered shame in exile for you, and at the hands of that same mad king my wife was taken from me and given to another man. While serving you, my own men have wanted to blame and kill me for what someone else had done to their families. Why do you still punish me?" he cried out to the wind in anger.

A cool wind blew across his face, giving him a moment of clarity in his cries to God. David realized that he was the mad king that had chased the innocent Bathsheba, that she was now the one being forced to suffer in shame in exile. That Uriah was now the man whose wife had been taken away by the same mad king and given to another while serving him loyally, and finally, it was Bathsheba who would be killed by her own friends and family for something someone else did to her. How had he allowed this to happen?

David hung his head and remembered one of the opening lines in his *Lament of the Bow* that he wrote about Saul and Jonathan after their deaths[1]. "How the mighty have fallen!" David's heart felt heavy knowing that his dear friend Jonathan died defending his mad king father. He was loyal to David, yet also stayed loyal to his father to the end. David thought of Uriah and the friendship and loyalty he had displayed to David through everything. David let those thoughts of Uriah swirl in his head a moment as he tried to find the words of an apology that he could share with him about what he had done. There was this freeing moment in David's heart as he considered the idea of owning and confessing his sin and embracing whatever consequences it brought, but then the chains of fear and shame came rolling back into his thoughts, once again binding his mind and heart to them. *There must be another way!*

Ignoring the whisper of the spirit inside him, David wrestled with what he felt were the only two paths that he could take if he were to bring an end to this horrible situation. He determined that although it would have been the most righteous path to take, the path of confession and owning his sin would only bring shame and danger to the kingdom of Israel. The idea of a sinful king that could not be trusted by his people or his men would only create internal turmoil. He knew his enemies would take advantage of this opportunity and perhaps precipitate the defeat and subjugation of the people of Israel.

Another idea came to him while trying to find a way to avoid the wrath of Uriah should he find out what happened. David reasoned that it had only been weeks since his encounter with Bathsheba and knowing that some babies come early and others late in delivery, this plan was simple and for the most part innocent.

Acting quickly, he sent a letter to Joab, asking that Uriah the Hittite be sent to Jerusalem. His purpose was to meet with David and provide an update on the situation at Rabbah.

[1] 2 Samuel 1:17-27

Chapter 6
The road less traveled
(Nathan)

The endless steps that Nathan had taken up the massive tower in his dream had left him exhausted, yet he somehow knew the purpose of climbing the dark steps of the tower was just around the corner, a few more steps. As he finally stepped into the sunlight, he closed his eyes to the brightness of the sun and let his eyes adjust to the orange glow from behind his eyelids. A warm wind blew across his face and cooled his body as it permeated his tunic and carried away the sweat from his efforts.

Once his eyes adjusted, he slowly began to open them, taking in the incredible vision laid out before him. He felt he was higher than the heavens and the air was so clear that he could see in every direction and even to the very edge of the horizon. It was beautiful and majestic.

As he looked down from the tower, he saw two roads that led from the tower and disappeared into the horizon. Nathan could see that the road to his left was wide and paved and wound its way through a mostly flat plain of green grass. Instead of taking the time and work needed to remove any rock formations or hills in their way, he saw how the builders of the road had carefully built around them, sometimes even losing forward progression in the process.

To his right, Nathan could see the road was narrow, yet straight as it immediately began its climb up and over the mountain range in front of it. Instead of going around the rock formations and obstructions, the builders of this road had stopped to remove them, ensuring the road remained straight in its goal to carry its travelers to their destination.

As he looked over the edge of the wall and down to the origins of the roads before him, he saw a man standing at the crossroads in deep thought, as if deciding which direction to choose. Nathan immediately recognized the man. It was David. Although different, he remembered the previous dream he had about David and the dangerous choice that was before him and how he had made the wrong choice before. He still did not know what that choice was that David faced or even understand enough of it to interpret it for his King.

At first Nathan felt a sense of peace knowing the decision David faced was an easy one and felt confident he would take the correct road before him. Wondering where his journey would take David, Nathan glanced at the wide and easy road as it wound its way across the plains. However, the further the road progressed the more turns and direction changes it made and more importantly, from his vantage point he could see that the ultimate destination of the road disappeared into a dark and deadly swamp.

Nathan quickly glanced back at the narrow and more difficult road and followed its path over the rugged mountains. This one's destination did not end in a deadly swamp of darkness, but a bright, rich and beautiful green valley. The road would be more difficult to traverse at first, but the reward would be worth it.

Nathan nervously looked back down to where David stood and waited anxiously for his decision. After several minutes, David chose wisely and began his trek up the narrow road toward the rich reward it would carry him too, but then he stopped and stared at the hills before him. Nathan repeatedly yelled from the top of the tower to let David know he had made the right choice, but the height of the tower and the wind carried his words away from David's ears. Nathan's heart dropped as he saw David turn back and instead follow the wide and easy path across the plains.

Nathan knew he had to reach David while he was still near, so he turned to run back down the dark stairs he had climbed to reach this spot, but there no longer was a door or steps to follow. His heart raced and as he ran to the edge of the tower to try and warn him again, but instead of stopping at the edge, Nathan stumbled and fell over it and toward the ground below. As the wind and weightlessness gathered around him, he knew what waited for him at the end of the fall. He hoped that the noise of his fall would at least stop David from going down the path he had chosen, but as he tried to scream, he suddenly awoke to find himself once again safely in his bed.

He had learned from previous dreams that there was the traditional shift from a panic to the realization of his safety, then his breathing and heartbeat would eventually slow as his mind transitioned from dreamland to reality. "What are you telling me Lord?" he mumbled the question in prayer as he tried to understand his dream. He knew that he was always being prompted by the spirit with insights and wisdom far beyond his own abilities, but it seemed the dreams he had been having about David were increasing in number and clarity. Falling off a tower to his death was not something he enjoyed experiencing. *Do I go and once again share the dream with David?* He wondered and thought about the many times before where he had shared his dream with David, who then looked at him with concern as if he had gone mad. The more he tried to convince himself not to go, the more the dream kept repeating itself over and over in his mind.

"Yes Lord, I'll go," he said out loud and then climbed out of bed and proceeded to put on his cloak, sandals and belt before once again heading to the palace to see God's anointed.

Chapter 7
A loss of power
(Joab)

Joab held the note from David in his hand, now being crushed repeatedly at each concerned thought that passed through his mind. He tried to understand the deeper meaning of the request to have Uriah sent to Jerusalem to give a report on the situation there.

"I'm the General and leader of the army, why did he not ask for me?" He asked his brother and crumpled the paper again.

"Maybe he felt you were too valuable and needed here," Abishai replied. "I think you are reading way too much into this, brother. He did not ask me either and I don't feel slighted, although I would have enjoyed spending some relaxing time and getting a hot bath there," he said with a chuckle.

Joab shook his head at his brother's reply. "There is more to this, Abishai; I can feel it in my bones. Uriah is being prepared to take over the leadership of the army and David is deliberately rubbing it in my face," he replied as he watched his brother pick at the plate of dates on the table in front of them.

"Giving the leadership of the Lord's army to a Hittite? I didn't think that would ever happen," he said as he took a bite of one of the dates he had finally selected.

Joab's mind was racing and battling a hundred thoughts as he sat quietly across from his brother. David must still be angry because of how he and his brother had killed Abner without David's prior approval. Yes, there was a revenge aspect for killing Abner after he had killed Joab's brother in battle, but as a former general of Saul's army he was a potential threat to David's rule and needed to be removed, not only for David's sake but to protect his own position as well. Joab felt David had overreacted to the whole event and he was still angry with David for parading he and his brother around in sackcloth for the people to see while Abner was taken to be buried. He thought about the event and its ramifications and decided he would do it all again if he had to. David, as well as everyone else in Israel who knew them understood how valuable and influential he and his brother were, and that to cross them would be dangerous.

If Uriah's position were to grow, he and his brother would need to draw him closer within their circle of influence. If drawing him close did not work, they would need to either undermine his authority and influence within the army and with the people of Israel or if necessary, to find a way to permanently remove him.

Joab turned to look at his brother who apparently was no longer particular about which date to eat, as there were now only a few remaining on the once full plate. "Send word to have Uriah brought to our tent. Let us prepare him for his trip to Jerusalem," he said sternly and Abishai swallowed, nodded and then stood up, wiping his hands on his tunic.

"Anything in particular you'd like to achieve in the meeting?" Abishai asked with a raised eyebrow. Joab paused and seemed deep in thought for a moment, but then smiled.

"I think I have an idea, but I'd like to see his response to the invitation first," he replied and then reached for one of the few remaining dates left on the plate. Abishai nodded and left his brother to enjoy them.

Chapter 8
A strange invitation
(Uriah)

Although there were cultural differences between Hittites and Hebrews, the greatest challenge that Uriah faced in his relationship with the Hebrew people was with their language, both written and spoken. The meeting he had just had with Joab and his brother Abishai was a perfect example of the frustration. He had worked hard learning to speak the language since joining David and simple battle commands were easy enough, but intricate details or explanations were far more difficult, as Joab and his brother made clear.

Why had David requested him, he wondered as he walked back to his men to gather and pack his weapons and gear for the journey to Jerusalem. He was not sure if he should feel honored or nervous by the request. Was David questioning his loyalty to him or did he want to extend praise for it? From the body language, demeanor and line of questioning from Joab, Uriah was quite sure Joab was wondering the same thing.

At first, they had discussed how the troops under his command were doing, then they asked his perspective on the current siege efforts they had put in place around Rabbah. With his limited vocabulary, he affirmed that his men were ready and in good health and that unless the Ammonites had found a way to entice another nearby kingdom to join them, the chance of a breakout before the siege ended would be very unlikely. With scouts positioned along key roads and access points coming from any of the Ammonites' potential allies, he felt their chances of being surprised by them were small.

The more they spoke, the more confident and excited he felt about going to Jerusalem to meet with David. Although David had spoken to him many times in the past at meetings, Uriah had never spent such a focused and purposeful time with the king. He was a man after God's own heart they had told him about David, and Uriah wanted to learn how to imitate that quality. Uriah knew he would do almost anything to win David's approval and friendship.

Almost anything, he thought. What were his limitations should David ask that of him, he wondered? He knew he would kill for him in battle, as he had already proven. He would lead men into dangerous situations, but would he truly die for him? He thought of his former training under Hittite leaders before joining David. He knew of their corruption and selfish lives, sacrificing others and even shifting blame and punishment onto the innocent men beneath their leadership to protect their glory or honor and position. He had learned to fight for them, because that was what he was paid to do, but he would never sacrifice his life to cover their mistakes. That is why he left the Hittite army when he heard of David and his leadership example and the God he believed in and followed. A man whose heart is pure and loves his troops more than himself; that is a man worth fighting and dying for.

Jerusalem. Uriah thought of the great city of David and its protective walls and tall battlements. He then thought of Bathsheba and her beauty and love for him. He longed to hold and caress her when this war was over. During their last time together, they had spoken of having children together, but he said it would be best to wait until the risk of war was behind them and, more importantly, he wanted to be there to be a part of every aspect of being a father. They would teach their children how to love the God of Israel with all their heart, mind, soul and strength just as David did. They wanted to grow old together as they learned to embrace this new culture and teaching of God.

He looked out and saw his men gathered around his tent, each somehow finding paper and ink, each writing and handing him messages to take to Jerusalem to be delivered to their families, some having others write it for them. Some, he learned, were notes to worried parents, others to their wives, and some were to their children. Judging from the size of the various scrolls, some were short and to the point, others apparently had much to share with their loved ones.

"Yes, I will find someone who will deliver them to your family," he had promised each one. "Just make sure you put your name and family names of who are supposed to receive them on the outside of each one, so they know where to send them."

"You will recognize Ari's family; his wife looks just like him, beard and all," one of the soldiers said in jest about a member of their group and, excluding Ari, they all laughed at Ari's expense.

Uriah smiled at the humor and then patted Ari on the shoulder. "Pay no attention to them, I'm sure the God of Israel is far too kind to inflict such a curse on your wife or children," he said, hoping his poor understanding of Hebrew would not prevent the humor of his words being grasped. At first Ari smiled and nodded in appreciation, then glanced back at Uriah with a glare and shook his head as the rest of the men began laughing. They had understood the humor and even patted Ari on the shoulder in appreciation until he eventually began smiling again.

"Just make sure my letter is delivered to my *beautiful* wife!" Ari yelled over the laughter and handed Uriah his letter. Uriah smiled and nodded as he added Ari's rolled letter to his special bag of letters that was growing larger every moment.

Uriah thought of the short letter he had written to Bathsheba. As much as he wanted to see her during his visit to Jerusalem, he thought of all his men who had not seen their families for months. It did not feel right and honorable. *As one,* was the motto he repeated to himself as he wrestled with the difficult decision he had made to not see her. He unrolled the letter and read the words,

When word of my brief visit to Jerusalem reaches you, I will probably already be on my way back to Rabbah to rejoin my men. Please know that I love you more than life itself, and I cannot wait until we can be together again and start our family, but I could not look my men in the eyes upon my return to them knowing that I had embraced and held you while they had not had the company of their loved ones. I know you are safe there in Jerusalem and under the protection of our King. I will be with you soon, my love. Uriah.

He waved to his men and yelled as he departed, "Do not fight without me!" and then joined the wagons heading to Jerusalem, wagons that he knew would then return and bring the much-needed supplies to the army camped there in Rabbah. During the entire journey, he battled with his decision about not visiting Bathsheba. He had almost convinced himself to change his mind, but honor and love for his men brought him back to his original conviction. He cleared his mind and focused on the upcoming meeting. He could not wait to be in David's presence and learn from him.

Chapter 9
A strange encounter
(Nathan)

As he once again walked toward the Palace of David, Nathan could not help but think about the dreams he had been given the past few days. Some involved falling off a tower, another watching a storm in the mountains sending walls of water down its valleys toward a critical junction that would either send its destructive waters toward the city of Jerusalem, or away from it. Another was of him and a powerful and dangerous wolf staring at him with burning red eyes, as if waiting for a decision from Nathan. To the right, Nathan could see a lone young ram standing guard but unaware or unconcerned about the powerful threat behind it. To the left was the entire flock, also unaware of the danger of the wolf. Nathan tried to grasp which one to help or protect, but if he chose one, he knew the other would suffer. He was frozen in his dream and awoke before he had made his choice.

He rubbed his sleepless eyes and took a deep breath of the cool evening air trying to gather the energy needed for the evening meeting with David. The only good he could find with the dreams was that they were an incredible blessing and motivation in his prayer life. He had spent hours in prayer wrestling with each dream and asking for God's wisdom. He was still waiting for the answers.

As he came to the entrance of the palace, he nodded to the usual guards and passed into the inner guardroom on his way to see David when a voice whispered from the darkness of the sleeping area.

"Master prophet, may I ask a favor of you?" The voice in the darkness spoke in a strong accent and the strange title he to address him further indicated that he was not Hebrew. Nathan could see a tall muscular young man moving into the light of the hallway lanterns.

Nathan at first did not recognize him, as he was not one of the usual guards, and once he stepped into the light, it was obvious he was not of Hebrew decent, nor did his choice of clothing act as a disguise. He was also carrying a large cloth bag at his side. As his face was finally revealed by the light, Nathan smiled and nodded. "You are Uriah, one of David's men and trusted leaders, of course. How can I be of assistance to you?" Uriah seemed relieved at his response and held up the strange bag for Nathan to take.

"Thank you! I have letters to the family members of my men in Rabbah that need to be delivered, but I do not have the time nor the knowledge of where their family members reside. I did not want to ask my King to assist in such a menial task, but I have found no one else able or willing," Uriah explained in a heavy Hittite accent. As Uriah helped Nathan take hold of the bag, Nathan realized that Uriah misunderstood that his desire to assist him was not necessarily a "yes, I will do whatever you ask," but more a question of trying to understand the need and if he could help. Yet now, holding the bag that Uriah had pushed into his hands, Nathan now seemed committed to following through with the request.

Although Nathan was familiar with most of the families in Jerusalem, he also knew how difficult it would be to quickly find what appeared to be so many of them. As he held the bag in silence and saw the relief on Uriah's face, he nodded and smiled, "Of course. It is the least I can do to keep this *menial* task from the King's obligations," Nathan replied, hoping Uriah did not realize the sarcasm of his response. He was a servant of the people, and he should view nothing as menial when serving others. He then watched a relived Uriah head back to his sleeping cot in the darkness. Thinking about the innocence of the young man and his request, Nathan suddenly started thinking beyond the strange encounter.

"Why are you sleeping here and not at home with your wife and family?" Nathan asked as Uriah turned to step back into the light. Nathan could see his facial expression was serious as he glanced at the bag Nathan was holding.

"I could not bring myself to enjoy a pleasure my men could not," Uriah replied and then looked at the bag he had given Nathan. "I have a letter for my wife in there. Could you please see that she receives it, but only after you have delivered the others?"

"Of course. Good night, Uriah," Nathan replied and watched the young soldier head back to his cot. Nathan could not help feeling the loyalty and honor the young man had to his men and the love and respect they must have for him. Holding the bag of letters, Nathan continued on to his planned meeting with David.

After waiting a short time outside David's reception area, Nathan was escorted into the room.

"Nathan, it is always good to see you," David said as Nathan approached.

"My King, it is always good to be in your presence. You seem to be in good spirits," Nathan replied, and David nodded.

"Yes, I just received a detailed report that our careful plans and objectives are working as planned in Rabbah. It might be a long siege, but it will minimize the loss of our soldiers' lives should we try to attack their walls," David replied and smiled and then his expression became more serious as he looked at Nathan's face. "How is your sleep my friend? Are those dreams still disturbing you?" David asked.

At first, Nathan hesitated. He did not want to burden David with another discussion around his strange dreams, but then he felt it might be important. "They are still there my lord, almost as if they are trying to tell me that I am missing something important," he replied, and David nodded as if trying to find an answer. Nathan could see that David was interested, so he continued. "It's as if we, you and I, are facing an important decision, or perhaps it is a series of decisions, that need to be made. If handled incorrectly, it could bring a great deal of harm to many people," Nathan replied. David seemed to shift into a deep thought. "Is there something I need to know or a decision that needs my advice and counsel for you?" Nathan asked bluntly. The question seemed to wake David out of his thoughts. After a few moments David replied.

"There are a hundred, perhaps thousands, of important decisions a king must make every day, so your dreams and questions do not surprise me. I believe I have taken the best path or made the right decision in each one I have been faced for the protection of the people of Israel." David said with a heavy smile and then glanced at the bag Nathan was holding. "What gift do you bring me?" David asked, changing the direction of the discussion.

At first confused, Nathan looked down at the bag in his hand and he remembered the story behind it. "It is a bag of letters from Uriah's men. Uriah asked me to deliver them to their families." David seemed surprised and uncomfortable by Nathan's response.

"Why did you go and see Uriah?" David asked in a concerned and almost accusatory voice. Nathan was surprised by the question but tried to clarify his answer.

"I did not visit him, my King. He was downstairs in the barracks with your servants when he approached me. He asked if I would deliver these and handed me the bag before I could decline, it's the least I could do for one of your men." At first, David seemed relieved at his answer, then confused.

"What do you mean he was in the barracks?" David asked.

"He said he felt he could not enjoy the company of his own family while his men could not," Nathan answered cautiously, feeling as if he was walking into a trap. David seemed confused by the response, but then after a moment regained his composure.

"He is a good soldier," David replied. "An honorable decision, to be sure."

"He reminds me a great deal of another man I know," Nathan said, thinking of David, and waiting for David to grasp the meaning. Either he chose not to, or it did not come to mind.

"I'm glad to hear you are better, my friend. I have a great deal on my plate; is there anything else you need from me before I get back to it?" David asked with a dismissive tone that Nathan easily grasped. It was such a quick change of tone and direction, that Nathan was caught off guard and instead of pursuing it, shook his head and bowed.

"No, my King. I shall leave you to it and pray for your success," Nathan replied and turned to leave.

"Sleep well, Nathan," David said. As Nathan was met and escorted through the main door, he could not help feeling the stress and pressure that David was apparently feeling. He wondered how the dreams he was having somehow related to them. As he passed the outer doors, he smiled at the thought of Uriah and his love for his men and loyalty to David. Yes, he did remind Nathan of David; a man after God's own heart.

Chapter 10
A broken strategy
(David)

David's plan had been so simple; have a brief meeting with Uriah, then send him home to be with wife Bathsheba. David's fist pounded the desk before him in anger and frustration. With so much time between a husband's last visit, what man could resist the desires for his wife in bed? More importantly, it would have created the alibi he needed to hide his encounter and it's outcome with Bathsheba. His carefully laid plan had failed.

David's mind raced as he tried to find a solution to remedy its failure. He had sent Uriah home for the night with orders to return to Rabbah the next day. David knew that time was short, and he would need more of it if he was to find a way to succeed. For the next few hours, he sat at his desk alone thinking of a solution to his unsolved problem. He wrestled briefly with the thought of bringing Uriah in, with an armed escort in case things turned violent, and confessing what he had done and asking for his forgiveness. David understood that was the quickest way to end the problem, but the fears and shame of his sin once again drove the thought from his mind.

Now that his mind was a little clearer, David understood who Nathan was talking about. Uriah was like a younger and, unfortunately, a more honorable him. His heart was heavy at the thought of how much he had changed since pursuing his path of sin with Bathsheba. He also knew exactly why Nathan was having those dreams and what they had meant when he had shared each one with him. He was continually facing the very choice he was facing now. But would he finally take the correct path? Is this the lesson that God was trying to get him to understand?

David began walking around his huge desk, circling it as if hoping to find a hidden path that would break him from the vicious and unending loop. He suddenly stopped at the front of his desk. If God's intention had been for him to learn his lesson, then God's purpose was fulfilled. Feeling such guilt and shame these past few weeks, he knew he would never do it again. With that thought, he struggled to find the peace he so desired. Then, as if it was a gift from God, the solution came to him.

Although he had a restless night's sleep, David went to the barracks early the next morning as if checking on the welfare of his men. With a lantern in one hand and two guards attending to him David walked into the barracks. As he had assumed, for it was what he would have done, Uriah was already awake and packing for his trip home.

"Uriah, why are you here? Why didn't you go home?" David asked Uriah, as if he did not know the answer already. Seeing the king, Uriah bowed and replied.

"The ark and Israel and Judah are staying in tents, and my men are camped in the open country. How could I go to my house to eat and drink and make love to my wife? Surely as you live, I will not do such a thing!" Uriah replied humbly.

Although Nathan had told him the reason Uriah had stayed in the barracks, the reality and deeper meaning of his words cut David like a knife. While all his men were in Rabbah, David had stayed in Jerusalem and done the very things that Uriah said he would never do, including sleeping with Uriah's wife. For a moment, David considered falling at Uriah's feet and begging for his forgiveness, ending this horrible charade, but then his plan came back to his mind. David nodded and grasped Uriah on the shoulder. "You are a good and honorable man. Stay here one more day, and tomorrow I will send you back," David stated. He could see that Uriah was wrestling with the invitation and probably the renewed temptations that he would face if he stayed, so David turned the invitation into an order. "That is an order soldier," David said with a smile and Uriah bowed to him.

"As you wish my King," Uriah replied without looking up.

"I want you to join me for food and drink this afternoon, just you and me in your honor," David stated, and he could see Uriah was torn between excitement and the compromise of his personal vows. "I will send one of my assistants to escort you to my office when the time comes. In the interim rest and relax, my friend," David ended, and he could see the pride and honor Uriah felt at being extended such a request, but the personal struggle he faced as well by accepting it. Once again Uriah simply bowed and nodded.

"Thank you, my King," was all Uriah said and did not look up.

David smiled as he released Uriah's shoulder and began walking toward the barracks door and back to his office. He felt relieved that the first step of his new plan would was a success. His heart felt heavy knowing that it would not have succeeded had he not ordered Uriah to attend. Somehow victory seemed to be within grasp again as he had succeeded in getting him to compromise on the eating and drinking part of his vow. If things went as planned this afternoon, the 'not making love to my wife' vow would be the final compromise.

Although David entertained many visitors and addressed many issues during the morning and early afternoon, his mind was focused on how he was going to guide Uriah down a path that would ultimately end in his wife's bed. It was not until the moment Uriah was being escorted into his meeting room that he realized that his deceitful plan was the exact same one that he had successfully used on Bathsheba. He was torn between feeling that he would essentially be reliving that moment, and the relief and confidence that his plan would work again and end this horrible consequence once and for all.

Chapter 11
A battle of wills
(Uriah)

Uriah's heart was heavy as he sat on his cot and thought about the request he had received from David. He was honored beyond his wildest dreams to be invited to another private meeting with David, however this meeting was in direct conflict with his personal vow. The first day was easy enough as he only ate the types of food given to the palace guards that matched what his men would be eating. He knew it had been long time since his last glass of wine, so avoiding the drinking side of his vow was his concern. However, he felt that if he addressed it from the position of a fellow warrior and leader, he was confident that David would understand.

With regards to his accommodations in the palace and that of his men, he was sure that the stuffy and smelly cots in the barracks were far less appealing than the open aired ground he and his men shared in their tents. Although he felt confident about overcoming the first three vows he had made, it was the increasing pull on his heart for the company of his wife and the vow he had made about her that he was now most concerned about breaking.

Uriah had tried to clean up his uniform as best he could before the meeting, but there was only so much to be done for worn leather and wool. After placing his weapons, wrapped in his cloak, under his cot he waited for the king's assistant to escort him to the presence of his king. He once again passed by the shields and weapons of fallen enemies hanging on the walls, along with the various works of art, either given or captured, sitting on tables or in alcoves. As he approached the door to the King's meeting room, he took a deep breath and slowly exhaled as he entered the chamber.

David was sitting behind a large table; Uriah was escorted to another chair sitting across the table from David's. The table was covered with some of the choicest of foods, many he had never seen before, and urns filled with an assortment of beverages from across the lands. In front of the chairs were various plates, cups, glasses and utensils to be used to consume the vast meal before them. There were two beautiful female servants standing at the ends of the table as if waiting for a gesture or command.

"Uriah! It is good to have you join me. How was your day?" David asked and motioned for Uriah to have a seat. As Uriah sat down, he tried to find anything on the table that would come close to matching the food his men would be eating this evening but could find nothing.

"It was good my King, time for plenty of prayer and reflection as the prophets advise," Uriah replied and smiled nervously.

"You visited Nathan today?" David asked, seeming concerned.

"No, my King, I did just what I've heard and was advised to do to draw closer to the God of the Hebrews," he replied in a serious tone. Uriah felt unsure about how to act from this point forward but wanted David to trust and believe in him. David nodded to one of his servants and she filled a cup and placed it in front of Uriah. As Uriah was about to raise his hand to refuse the cup, David proposed a toast.

"To Uriah, my greatest warrior and trusted friend!" David cheered and raised his glass to Uriah. Uriah felt like a deer caught in a trap that he could not break free from. If he refused the toast to honor his personal vow, he would be rejecting the King's kind words, yet if he drank of it, he would break one of them. "I feel blessed to have you in my service," David added to his toast and drank the whole cup. The additional kind words became the tipping point as to what Uriah should do. He reached over, took the cup and followed his King's example, drinking down the entire beverage. Uriah immediately knew that it was not the wine or ale that he expected, but a much stronger drink. It burned his throat going down and filled his nostrils to the point of almost causing him to cough.

As Uriah set his cup down, one of the servants immediately began to fill it again. Unable to speak just yet due to the fading burn from the previous drink, Uriah tried to wave off the servant with his hand, but David once again raised his own cup and made another toast.

"To the brave men that you lead!" David said and drained his cup again and slammed it on the table with a bang and a smile. Uriah looked at the cup and thought about his men and the toast that honored them. *Just one more,* he thought, and picked up the cup pouring the burning liquid down his throat again. Although the beverage came from the same container, this one seemed to burn more than the previous one and he once again fought the urge to cough. As if on cue, the cup was refilled, and a new toast was shouted by David.

"To the beauty and honor of our wives, may God always protect them!" David shouted and drank the third cup as he had done with the previous ones, except this time he set it gently on the table. Uriah hesitated, still trying to recover from the previous two toasts, and then looked up at David to see a concerned look at his delayed mutual toast. Uriah held up his hand as if asking for a moment as he tried to gather his thoughts but realized that the longer the pause continued during this moment, the more awkward the moment became. He smiled and picked up his cup and drained it. To his surprise, the third cup went down much easier than the previous two.

"To the glory and beauty of our wives, and men and friendship," Uriah replied hoarsely, then grasped his poor word choice in Hebrew and tried to correct it. "Not to the beauty of our men, but our wives and to their bravery," he mumbled his correction, then realized he had repeated the error again. "Not to the bravery of our wives, but to, not that they aren't brave…" he stumbled to a stop and felt foolish and embarrassed at what could only be an offense to his king. After a brief pause David suddenly burst into laughter and smiled at Uriah.

"Yes, it would take a great deal of bravery to marry us," David slapped the table with his hand and continued. "Despite your heavy accent and brave attempt at Hebrew, I knew what you meant, Uriah." David ended and smiled as he let his laughter slowly fade. "You must be hungry, please eat," David said and pointed at the vast amount of food the was spread out before him.

As the three toasts coursed their way through his stomach and into his blood and brain, he realized it was the first chance he had to explain his situation and vows. "My King, it was my desire to refrain from both drink and eating of anything my men did not have, to honor them," Uriah explained while David listened attentively. "I feel in honoring your toasts, I have failed in the first one," he ended somberly. Uriah watched as David sat in silence yet nodding at Uriah's response. Uriah could not help feeling the alcohol slowly working its way into his blood and thoughts. *Surely it must be doing the same to David*, he was thinking when David broke the silence.

"I'm sorry I have played a role in affecting your personal vow. So, in support of your vow and men, I will send along a barrel of ale for them to enjoy as well. In fact, pick one of these delicacies that you would like to eat this evening, and I will make sure to send along enough for your men to enjoy as well," David pledged and waited for Uriah's response.

At first stunned, Uriah suddenly felt proud of the moment, knowing that his men would soon be enjoying what was laid out before him and the drink that was now flowing through his blood. *What an incredible blessing,* he thought and then realized he had not returned the honor of a toast to David.

"To King David, the greatest King of Israel!" he shouted and then drained his cup again, slamming it on the table as David had, which David humbly honored by drinking his in return. Although somewhat of a blur, Uriah remembered the rest of the evening as being one filled with laughter, stories and many more toasts. David seemed untouched by the many toasts, but after the 5th or 6th one, Uriah did not seem to care. Toward the end of the meeting, while it was still light out, David suggested to Uriah what seemed to make perfect sense.

"Go home to your wife and enjoy the warmth of her touch and the feel of her body," David said, but Uriah started shaking his head and mumbling about his vow. However, David then continued. "Not to worry my friend. To honor your vow, I will see that your men are rotated back to Jerusalem at the earliest opportunity to enjoy the same pleasure you will have tonight. That gift will make you an even greater hero and friend to them," he said with a serious look and a smile.

Uriah could not believe the incredible gift that David had offered to his men and to him. The thought of holding Bathsheba in his arms, kissing her lips and loving her after such a long time was an incredible blessing that only a great King could give to a soldier. He nodded at the thought and David must have seen it, as David suddenly stood up and addressed Uriah directly.

"Go home and spend tonight with your wife, my friend. I will have my assistants gather the ale and food for your departure back to Rabbah in the morning." David ordered. Uriah felt honored and overwhelmed by, not only the meal and time with David, but the gifts for him and his men. Although it was difficult from the strong drink, Uriah struggled to his feet and nodded to David.

"Thank you, my King. That is the greatest gift you can give a man, or that I could pass along to my men. Good night." Uriah fought against the shifting floors and walls as he worked his way to the doorway. He could hear David give an order and then two guards stepped into the room.

"Would you be so kind as to help our guest to his home?" David ordered and the two men nodded and moved to Uriah's side and helped him navigate through the door, then the stairs, and down the grand hallway to the palace doors. As Uriah was passing the barracks, he remembered his weapons and gear under his cot and raised a hand for them to stop.

"I need to get my things," Uriah mumbled, and the two soldiers honored his request and stepped back as Uriah moved to the door of the barracks and to his designated cot. Not trusting his balance, he awkwardly sat down on his cot and reached under it to retrieve the bundle. Although his mind was foggy, his reasoning for needing his items was not. He was a soldier, and you never leave your weapons and equipment behind. They were a part of you, just like your men were a part of you. As he unrolled it, he looked at the sword, his dagger and the traveling pack that had been his life the past ten years and paused. *Had been?* Uriah thought and contemplated that piece of his internal discussion. He shook his head to clear it. "I am still a soldier and would remain one until I am killed in battle or released from the King's service?" he mumbled in his native language.

Still sitting on his cot, he felt the effect of his current inebriated condition. Had he lost David's respect this evening? David was truly a warrior who seemed unaffected by the strong drink. He thought of Bathsheba and how he longed to see and hold her this evening. He then thought of his men and how they would soon be holding their wives and families too and enjoying the same delicious drink and food he had experienced. Reaching for his sword, Uriah suddenly felt the strong drink try to move the cot underneath him and he sat up to regain his balance. He took a deep breath and looked around, seeing his two escorts still waiting for him at the entrance. He could see they were finding his current condition amusing and the reality of it saddened his heart. *How could he let his wife see him in this condition, let alone make love to her?* he asked himself, embarrassed even by the thought.

In a moment of clarity, he shook his head and decided his next course of action. He motioned to the two guards, who moved to where he was sitting. "I will be staying here this evening, so your assistance is no longer needed. Thank you," he ended. The soldiers seemed either relieved that they would not be responsible for carrying him home, or in agreement with his decision.

Uriah slid his sword and equipment back under the cot with his foot and laid carefully back onto it as if it were going to somehow slide out from underneath him. Once settled and secure, he thought of Bathsheba, his love for her and the missed opportunity to see her. He also thought of the incredible gift and blessing of spending time with his King. He closed his eyes and sleep came quickly.

Chapter 12
A even darker path
(David)

David felt at peace knowing that his problem was now behind him. He had given one of the guards escorting Uriah home a note signed by him to give to Bathsheba that simply said, "Welcome your husband home with open arms and devotion." He was sure she would understand the meaning of it and the opportunity it presented. Even if by chance Uriah were to read it first, he would see it as David keeping his promise to him. David was confident that whether Uriah slept through the evening, which was understandable in his condition, or did his best to fulfill his duty as a husband, Bathsheba would help convince Uriah how the moment was not wasted, enabling them both the deniability they needed.

He had to admit that even drinking the diluted version of the drink that Uriah consumed with each toast, he could feel the results. He wondered how Uriah had lasted as long as he did and was grateful when the loss of control point finally arrived so that he could end the charade. David was not proud of the evening but enjoyed knowing that things unfolded as he had planned. He had more admiration for Uriah now than before. He was loyal, a man of deep convictions, a great example of a personal leader of men, a man he could trust and a great warrior. He made a note that he would bring him closer to his inner circle of men guiding and leading the people of Israel. David sighed and shook his head. He deeply regretted all that had happened and once again committed to never following that path again.

Late that evening as he was returning from a dinner meeting outside the Palace, he saw one of the guards who had escorted Uriah home. "Shalom Rani, how is our guest Uriah?" he asked with a smile.

"He is sleeping well, my King," Rani replied, and David nodded as they passed, then David turned and asked another question.

"Did you deliver the note I gave you to his wife?" David asked and Rani reached into his pocket and took out the note and handed it to David.

"No, my King. Uriah insisted on sleeping in the barracks again," he replied. David's heart sank in shock at the news, and he walked back to where Rani was standing.

"I ordered you to take him home!" David hissed angrily and Rani seemed surprised by David's rebuke. Rani swallowed and then lowered his head.

"Apologies, my King, I did not know it was an order, but a request to assist him to where he wanted to go, which we did," Rani replied humbly, then continued. "Shall we go and wake him and carry him to his home?"

David tried to not only find the right response to Rani's question, but a solution to the problem that did not seem to want to die. The idea of waking Uriah out of a deep drunken sleep this late at night and dragging him home did not seem wise, especially considering it was Uriah's choice to stay. David fought to control his panic and fear of seeing his plans unravelling before his eyes. *Curse you Uriah, your honor will ruin us all,* David thought as he clenched his fists and tried to think of what should be done. He could see that Rani was waiting for a reply, still holding the note in one hand. "No Rani, it was not an order. Just what I thought would be best for Uriah." David said and reached out and took the note. "Sleep well tonight," David replied and smiled. Rani nodded and bowed, then turned and continued on his way. David's mind raced as he stumbled numbly up the various stairs and hallways to his chamber, finally ending with his sitting on the end of his bed, staring out the door that led to the balcony where this horrible and unfortunate situation all started.

David had felt the hand and Spirit of God guiding and directing him for so many years that he had forgotten what it felt like when it was not there. David felt lonely and fearful as he now faced this challenge alone. He had prayed and asked God to find a path out of this sin, one that would protect the nation of Israel from the embarrassment and shame, but none had been revealed to him. Although there was a part of him that wanted to just expose and confess the sin, he knew that as a man after God's own heart, he knew that God had the same heart and mind as his about protecting his people. David knew that God could not be involved in the solution and was leaving it in David's hands to solve. It was not easy being King, and the decisions you needed to make would sometimes cost the lives of men, women, children and families to achieve them. *Seek the needs of the kingdom first*, he thought and nodded. It was his responsibility to make the difficult decisions needed to protect the kingdom.

Embracing the freedom that a *kingdom first* mindset provided, David's next plan came easily. It was dark and sad in many ways, but he knew it would bring the ending and solution that was needed. What he needed to determine was how many people he should involve in it. He needed to find someone who was either loyal to him and the kingdom, or someone who desired and enjoyed embracing the power of leadership and further securing his position within it. One name immediately jumped into his head. Joab.

David knew the costs and benefits of inviting Joab into this plan. On one hand, it would give Joab leverage and power over him should he ever need to request a favor or counter a threat to his position. However, involving him in this plan would also give David more power and control over Joab as well. They would be tied together in this until their deaths or the discovery of their secret. The greatest risk for David was the possibility that Joab, as second in command of the army, would take a stand against the plan[1]. Perhaps revealing it to Uriah, to his brother, or other leaders, using it to overthrow David's kingship.

David thought long and hard about that possibility, but he knew that the men were loyal to him. Yes, they feared Joab, but they loved David as did the rest of the nation of Israel. David was also the anointed of God. With that power, he could deny that he had written or given the orders, turning the tables on Joab. David knew that there would be the danger and risk of losing the trust of the army and leaders, but he felt he could win them back with time. David knew that he would still have to ultimately deal with the 'with child' issue of Bathsheba, which Joab currently knew nothing about. However, once Uriah was removed, it would not matter. David even had a plan for that situation. Yes, Joab would be the person.

David smiled and took a deep breath as he wrote the orders for Joab and then sealed it in a protective tube. It seemed ironic that Uriah would be carrying the orders to the leader who would arrange for his death. His heart was heavy as he reminded himself that it was best for the kingdom and that it would be the final act of this unfortunate situation.

[1] 2 Samuel 3:38-39

Chapter 13
A lingering doubt
(Nathan)

Nathan had considered passing the responsibility of delivering the letters to the respective families that Uriah had given him to one of his assistants, but he had given Uriah his word that he would take care of the matter. He had been impressed by Uriah's loyalty and respect for his men by asking that their letters to their spouse and families be delivered before his own. Although it was respect and honor that Nathan felt, it was Uriah's clear love for his soldiers that impressed him the most.

Although it had taken several days to personally deliver all the letters, and he was on his way to deliver the last one as promised, he was happy and encouraged by his decision. He was confident that it had been God's will for him to deliver those letters, not only requiring him to personally go among the people and learn and pray about their needs, but to his surprise, be blessed in having his own cup filled in doing so. At almost every stop, he was invited in and treated to delicious meals and friendly discussions, and also often being offered something to take back home, which was a marked improvement on what he would normally have eaten.

It was not just the blessing of the meals, he also felt more connected to the people. It had even helped him improve his social skills and confidence, something he was advised he needed to work on as a younger man of God. It had helped him further develop a Godly understanding of empathy and compassion. He was sad that this would be his last delivery on this enjoyable journey.

Finding Uriah's home was easy, as it was next to the king's palace. As he knocked on the door and waited for a response, he glanced up at the palace. The evening sunset cast an orange tint on the western side of the building and Nathan was surprised to see David looking down from what he was sure was the balcony that led from his bedroom. He waved at the king, but David must not have seen him and turned and stepped back from the edge of the balcony and into his room. Nathan was lowering his hand from the unanswered wave when the door suddenly opened.

Nathan was surprised to see a rather stern-faced woman glaring angrily at him from the narrow opening on the other side of the door. "How may I assist you?" she asked sternly and protectively at first and then seemed to soften her tone after apparently recognizing the prophet who stood before her. "Forgive me, my lord. Please come in," she said and fully opened the door, stepping back to make room for Nathan to enter.

"Shalom," Nathan replied and moved across the threshold and into the entry area beyond the door, happy to be out of the evening heat. Of all the letters he had delivered, he had never felt nervous or strange about delivering them until now. He glanced around the room and was surprised by the simplicity, but high quality of the furnishings. He glanced back at the woman and then realized he had yet to explain his purpose for his visit. "Yes, umm… Could you please inform the lady of the house that I have come to deliver a letter from her husband Uriah," Nathan added and then felt a little embarrassed as he was confident that she knew the name of her mistress's husband. "He asked me to give this to her, after first delivering the letters from the rest of his men to their families," again, he awkwardly stumbled over his words, not sure why he felt the need to explain his reason for delivering her letter last. He tried to take a deep breath to help calm his mind. He could not put his finger on why he felt so awkward or why even now she looked as if she was waiting for something. She then bowed her head and smiled.

"Please wait here while I notify my mistress that you wish to give her the letter personally," she said and headed toward the closest inner doorway and up a set of stairs. Nathan exhaled his held breath and realized that in his nervous state he had never offered the letter to her. He thought about calling out to have her come back and take the letter from him, but not only was she too far away to see, but he was concerned he would just say or do something else that would further embarrass him. He shook his head and paced nervously as he waited.

Several minutes later Bathsheba, followed closely by her servant, came down the stairs toward the room where Nathan was waiting. Although he had seen her before in social settings, he had never been this close to her or had ever spoken to her personally. Her beauty was stunning, and Nathan knew that Uriah was a very fortunate and blessed man. Strangely enough, he was far less nervous speaking to Bathsheba than he was to the servant. In fact, he was almost relaxed again.

"Shalom," Bathsheba said as she entered the room and bowed her head to the prophet, "Talia informed me that you had a letter from my husband. Is he well?" she asked with deep concern in her voice. As he started to reply, he noticed that her arrival carried a rare but familiar scent into the room with her. He tried to remember where he had recently last smelled that rare fragrance but could not. Disregarding the thought, he returned the bow and smiled.

"Shalom. Thank you for seeing me. I know of no illness or any other reason for you to have concern for your husband. I am only here to bring a letter he left with me during his recent visit to Jerusalem," he replied.

"Uriah is here in Jerusalem?" She asked and Nathan could not tell if she was excited or nervous about the possibility.

"No, he was here two days ago. He had a meeting with King David," Nathan replied, but was surprised by her reaction. Instead of being sad that she missed Uriah, she seemed nervous about Nathan's response.

"What was the meeting about?" she asked and moved closer to Talia for comfort, or was it for protection, Nathan wondered.

"I'm afraid I do not know or can share all the details, but it was primarily an update on the war with the Ammonites. What I do know is that he asked that I deliver the letters from his men to their families first and yours last," he ended with a smile and Bathsheba smiled.

"That sounds like something Uriah would do, put the needs of his men's family before his own," she said with a faint smile. He is an honorable man," she added.

"Yes. I saw the same quality in him," Nathan said and then handed her the letter that he had been carrying around the past two days. Bathsheba nervously reached out and took the letter and slowly opened it and began reading it. Nathan thought about excusing himself but did not want to interrupt her moment with her husband's personal letter. As he watched her read the letter, her eyes filled with tears and Talia reached out to touch her arm. At first, he thought the tears were joyful tears, but then to his surprise they seemed to change into something different as she finished reading it, almost as if they were tears of sadness. "Is everything all right?" he asked her, concerned that something horrible was said in the letter. She looked up from the letter and nodded her head.

"Yes, it was kind of you to deliver this. Would you excuse me?" she asked but did not wait for an answer before turning and heading back toward the stairs. "Would you be so kind as to offer our guest a drink or meal in appreciation for his service?" she said softly to Talia who was trying to follow her up the stairs. Talia stopped briefly to glance back at Nathan, but Nathan did not wait for the offer.

"Thank you, but I must be going," he said and headed for the door, putting his hand up as Talia started to walk toward the door as well. "I will let myself out. Shalom," he said and opening the lever and stepping back out into the street. All the letters he had delivered prior to this one had been happy, joyous, and filled with gratitude and conversation. He thought the last visit would be the best one, not the worst.

Nathan took a deep breath of the fresh, unperfumed air as he walked down the side road that went past the palace toward his home. He suddenly realized when and where he had last smelled the fragrance of cinnamon, it was the late night he had the horrible dream about David and had rushed to the palace in fear that something had happened to him. A strange feeling hit him, and he stopped walking and looked around the area. He then realized that this was the exact spot where he had passed the two women, that night, both hiding behind their cloaks and smelling of cinnamon.

As he tried to revisit the image of those two women that night, he realized their similarities to Talia and Bathsheba. Nathan felt frozen in place as he wrestled with what he was supposed to do with that suspicion. After several moments, he finally shook his head determining it was not his concern and continued toward home. Several turns and long stretches later, he had still not let go of the question that was trapped in his mind. "What were you two doing that night?" Nathan asked out loud before opening the door to his home.

Chapter 14
A life in your hands
(Joab)

Joab could not remember how many times he had reread the unsigned letter from David before finally watching the flames consume the paper as ordered. He considered keeping it for leverage should things go poorly for him, but with the king's seal on the protective tube, instead of on the letter itself, no one would believe him. Everything seemed wrong about the orders. The king had sent Uriah back with a wagon full of food and drink to honor him and his men, yet at the same time issuing a death warrant for him.

What had David discovered about Uriah, that prompted him to direct Joab to arrange Uriah's death? Joab paced back and forth within his tent seeking a clue. What did David know that he did not? If Uriah were a spy, he would have had him arrested and killed on the spot. Joab knew Uriah's love and loyalty to David was without question, so what could it be? Joab searched his thoughts and even ventured into his own darkest schemes of power but could find nothing that could be applied to Uriah. Had he somehow offended or threatened David during his time in Jerusalem? Again, as hard as it would be to believe, even if he had, he never would have been allowed to return to the protection of his men.

What an odd twist of fate, Joab thought and smiled. The whole time Uriah was in Jerusalem, all Joab could think about was how to undermine Uriah's favored position with David and his potential threat to Joab's own leadership. Now David was asking him to not only reduce Uriah's influence but have him killed. Joab felt that perhaps God was finally rewarding him for his loyalty to David and the people of Israel by elevating him to the top position. His heart felt conflicted at the thought of how difficult it will be to find a replacement for Uriah, who was one of his most effective and respected leaders under Joab's authority. *I'm just following orders*, Joab reminded himself, knowing the details of a replacement well sort themselves out later.

As he continued thinking about options for seeing Uriah removed, the thought of Uriah's men was a serious concern and their potential deadly reaction if his removal was not handled with extreme care. Joab knew that every one of them could be a threat to his leadership and even his life if Uriah's death was traced back to him. A thousand options raced through his mind before he finally decided that, Uriah's men must be removed as well. He had enough potential threats out there, most would like to see him dead for past decisions he had made in his pursuit of power and leadership. *But how can I remove both Uriah and his men at the same time?* He wondered.

Then he realized that David had already provided him with the answer in his letter.[1] At first Joab had discounted David's suggested idea of sending Uriah to the front where the fighting was fiercest and then pulling back. After all, the plans for taking this last Ammonite fortress city were based around a long-term siege, not a frontal attack. Uriah and his men were far too experienced as fighters to allow themselves to be caught exposed or trapped in the open, and unless the Ammonite general was an idiot, getting the Ammonites to leave their protected walls to attack him would not happen, no matter how attractive the bait might be. Joab walked back to his desk and for the hundredth time studied the hand drawn map of the city and its fortifications. Except this time, instead of studying it from the perspective of finding the best way to take the city with the least losses, he tried to find an approach that would not only inflict the most losses for his men, but to then trap them there, or to be more precise, Uriah and his men.

Joab knew that unless he had a more complete plan that would convince Uriah that he and his men would be safe and protected during this high-risk attack, he would never agree to it, nor would any of the other leaders. The back story of the 'change of strategy' in the taking of the city would have to be very convincing, detailed, and a sound potential for success. If not, the attack plan would be rejected and overruled by his other leaders. It was several hours later that he worked out the details and back story of his plan and sent one of his assistants to find his brother. If he could convince him, then he felt confident he could get the rest of the leaders, even Uriah, to agree on the plan.

At first Abishai shook his head in disagreement as Joab explained his new plan to take the city and end the siege quickly. It was not until Joab had said that that the new plan was David's suggestion that Abishai was less adamant against it and even willing to consider it. "Although it has the potential for a quick victory, there are too many opportunities for things to go wrong. Brother, if this goes poorly, you do not want to have this defeat attached directly to you," he said without looking up from the map. Joab let an unseen smile cross his face as he heard his brother's response, knowing that the first part of his plan was working. Shifting the blame and consequences of his actions onto someone else was something he had practiced often in life, and it had often helped him avoid the full blame of his personal actions.

Abishai suddenly started shaking his head and smiling, "You have to respect David and his faith when it comes to battle. He always leans into and relies on his trust in God. This could finish the war quickly and bring the men home to their families early. They will sing even more songs about his prowess and leadership when this one is over," Abishai said, in an almost disappointed tone. "Uriah and his men will also gain a great deal of honor and respect," Abishai said with the same tone and took a deep breath as he continued staring at the map in front of him.

Although Joab's plan was coming together perfectly, Abishai's words of confidence in David, and not him, cut him deeply. He knew his brother did not know that David had nothing to do with the details of the plan before him, nor did he know the sinister purpose of it, yet he still believed in David's leadership ability more than his own brother's. Joab realized that he had thought through the plan so carefully, that the potential for its success was even greater than he expected, and he took pride in it.

He started wrestling with the idea of telling Abishai that David had nothing to do with the plan, that it was his alone and that he should get the honor and glory for the idea and the ultimate victory. He wanted the songs and stories to be written about him and not David. He allowed his mind to race down the various paths that would enable him to reveal the truth about the victorious plan.

However, after several minutes, he swallowed his pride and remained silent. As much as he wanted the recognition of the victory, he knew that the purpose of the plan was not victory, but defeat and the ending of Uriah and his men. Any other outcome would go against David's orders. Sadly, he somehow knew that if he spoke up and said it was his plan, like his brother had responded before he had given credit for the idea to David, the army would not follow or agree to it. If he remained silent and allowed it to be a victory, the glory and honor would go to Uriah and David, and he would be worse off politically than he was before the victory. The realization of it all stung his pride.

"Yes, David is quite the tactician and leader," he replied to his brother, who either missed or ignored the sarcasm in his tone. "Shall we gather the leaders and present the plan to them?"

Abishai nodded and then looked up from the map. "Your challenge is in convincing Uriah to be a part of this dangerous plan. I know I would never do it if I was asked," Abishai replied honestly and shrugged. Joab nodded.

"I agree. I know I would not either," Joab replied, but he already had a time proven strategy to overcome any objections Uriah might have.

---

[1] 2 Samuel 11:15

Chapter 15
A blind trust
(Uriah)

Although everything had gone according to plan up to this point, Uriah could not help feeling the hidden doubts he had in agreeing to put himself and men at such extreme risk. Two days ago the idea seemed so clear and glorious during Joab's presentation of the plan to the other leaders of the army of Israel. Even then he could see the same doubts in their faces regarding the extreme dangers and risks to the unit leading the attack, should the plan not go perfectly.

This unit would be 'the key to the lock of the city' is how Joab referred to it and everyone nodded in agreement, but no one, including Uriah, wanted the assignment. What made it so dangerous was that if the key did not fit the lock perfectly and exactly on time, there would be almost no chance of any members of the unit surviving. The plan was good, but everyone felt the risk was too high for that one unit. It was not until Joab made it clear that this was David's plan that Uriah had a change of heart toward it.

Looking back on it, Uriah knew that moment was the point in time when he allowed his personal pride and selfish ambition to overrule his common sense. Joab must have seen it too, for he proceeded to lavish praise and confidence in Uriah and his men, which further grew his pride while diminishing his sense of danger. The other leaders knew where this was heading and began nodding in agreement with Joab's assessment of Uriah and his men. The scales had tipped too far to one side for Uriah to see his way out.

The other leaders knew that if Uriah would be foolish enough to somehow embrace the assignment, they would not have to. He did not blame them, for he knew where it was heading as well. He could remember hearing what he could only describe as a silent scream of warning coming from somewhere in the back of his mind, the one that was still shouting. The scream was not from a fear of death at the hand of an enemy, nor from a lack of faith in his men and their ability to accomplish their part of the plan. The warnings and hesitations were his putting total trust and reliance in Joab and his guarantee to follow through with the rest of the plan as promised. Joab must have known that doubt would surface and silenced the scream with one statement.

"David said there was only one man that he felt confident enough in their abilities to lead this attack, you, Uriah," Joab had said, and the other leaders mumbled their agreement. Whatever warning that once held Uriah back was silenced by his growing pride in David's personal selection and confidence in him. "What response shall I tell the King?" Joab asked.

"Tell the King, my men and I will accept the honor," Uriah had replied and nodded with pride, but deep down the voice was still screaming its warning. From that point on, it was a gradual realization of the mistake he had made in listening to his pride. A mistake that could only be remedied by abandoning his pride in front of everyone, which that same pride would not allow him to do. He and his men were now trapped by it.

Pushing the now discouraging memory from his thoughts, Uriah tried to peer through the darkness of night to make out the faces of his men now hidden in the thick underbrush next to the designated section of wall of the Ammonite city where the start of Joab's plan was to unfold. Under the cover of darkness, they had spent the last four hours slowly and quietly crawling to this position, where they would rest before preparing to scale the wall just before first light. Although he was proud of his men for getting here without being discovered, he would not have been disappointed had one of them made a mistake that had gave away their plans before arriving, forcing them to retreat and end the danger.

Uriah could see that the faintest light of dawn was slowly driving away the darkness. That meant that he and his men were only moments away from launching their attack which, if successful, would quickly put the rest of the attack plan into motion. Only if the rest of the army was successful and timely, would it prevent the death of him and his men.

Essentially, their attack, and ultimately the taking of this section of wall, would be the bait they needed to draw the Ammonite defenders from nearby wall defenses so that the rest of the army could attack and overwhelm those sections of wall before the Ammonites discovered the ruse. Everything was about perfect timing. If the army of Israel attacked too soon, the Ammonite defenders would still be close enough to return to their original defenses before the Israelites arrived at the wall. If they attacked too late, then Uriah and his men would be overwhelmed by the mass of defenders shifting to regain the breached section of their wall defenses. If the timing were perfect, and only if it were perfect, it would create the distraction needed for the army of Israel to not only succeed in taking their nearby section of the city walls, but to then send the reinforcements needed to relieve Uriah and his men before they were overwhelmed.

Uriah knew there were too many variables for things to have perfect timing, but if they were at least close on the timing, he felt confident in his men's ability to hold the wall long enough to survive and even celebrate their victory. Even with perfection, he knew that he would lose men today. Perhaps with a victory they would all be back in Jerusalem by the end of the week. He started thinking about Bathsheba, but quickly drove thoughts of her from his mind. He needed to stay focused and alert.

Over the last three hours of darkness, Uriah's men had been quietly reassembling, wrapping and tying together the pieces of a ladder that they had carried with them. The ladder, once assembled, would be long enough to reach and secure the top of their section of the wall and strong enough to support at least four men climbing up it at the same time. It was the responsibility of the first soldier who reached the top to secure, protect and hold the wall. Then the second soldier climbing over would then do the same for the next and so on, until all the men had reached the more protected and defensible top of the fortress wall. The fading darkness would help hide them, but if they were discovered early, the archers from the nearby towers would be able to dispatch them faster than they could climb the ladder. Speed and stealth were essential, or the first few men arriving would be overwhelmed, which was why Uriah would be the first one up the ladder.

He tried to do a quick head count of his men in the darkness, but the most he could see in the undergrowth were, at best, 20 of his 40 men. Although there were 50 men that belonged to his unit, he felt the need to only take 40, partly because he did not feel more than 40 men could be concealed in the small area of underbrush they now occupied. The other reason was the strong doubt he could see in the eyes of the other 10. He knew doubt, like yeast, could expand through the rest of the unit.

At first, he was surprised when he realized that the majority of the 'doubting' 10 were the older men in his unit and he even quietly questioned their courage, but later he understood that their doubt had nothing to do with a lack of courage. It was fueled by a deep concern and love for the men and the knowledge of the incredible danger this plan put them all in. Had he valued and sought their subtle counsel instead of dismissing it, they probably would not be in the situation he and the rest of his men were now in. He wished he had their skills and wisdom with him now, somehow convincing him to turn back.

He knew the moment was at hand to begin the attack, but the voice of doubt that had been screaming from his heart was now louder than ever before, as if warning him that it was not too late. He felt embarrassed by the thought, knowing he had dismissed some of his own men for such doubt. He just wished someone would dismiss him and his men for the same doubt. His confidence should have been growing, as everything had gone perfectly from plan up to this point. So why the warning, he wondered. He was glad his men could not see the doubt in the darkness that was now overwhelming him.

Uriah glanced one last time through the brush, back toward the nearby hill where he knew Joab was watching the plan unfold. It was the last chance he felt they now had, hoping to see two torches being waved, signaling that the attack had been called off, but there was only darkness. He closed his eyes and said a short and silent prayer for himself and his men, and then moved to the front where the assembled ladder was waiting under cover.

Uriah nodded and watched as four of his men silently slid the cobbled-together ladder from the brush and approached the wall with it. As they had practiced countless times, with one fluid motion the base of the ladder was secured and held by two men, while the other two pushed and tipped it toward the top of the wall. They tried to slow the speed of its approach as the top reached the upper part of the wall, but Uriah could see that it would not be a gentle landing. Fortunately, they had wrapped the landing point of the ladder with cloth, so when it reached the wall, there was only a muffled thud. Uriah waited, almost wishing to hear the warning calls of their discovery to come from above, but there was only silence. He knew they were committed from this point forward.

With one fluid motion, Uriah and his men moved from their concealed location toward the wall. The four men who had positioned the ladder now did their best to hold it in place as the weight of the men flowed up it. There was a cowardly place in Uriah's heart that wished the ladder would break on his way up, but it held.

As he reached the top of the wall, he held the wall with one hand and pulled his sword with the other as he leaped over the battlements. He expected to be met by spears and arrows from the defenders, but there was no one waiting. He took up a defensive position, while sliding his shield off his back and into his left hand. With towers on both sides of where they had breached the wall, he expected missile attacks and warning shouts the moment they arrived, but again there was silence.

As more and more of his men reached the top of the wall and prepared themselves for battle, there was an incredible unexpected opportunity before him. Uriah knew the plan was to try to secure and hold one of the towers once they had secured the wall. Having secured the wall with no losses or even being discovered, he considered dividing his force and taking both towers. This would create the perfect pathway to move the whole army into the city and overwhelm the defenders, the very goal the other attacking army was to try to accomplish. However, Uriah dismissed the idea, knowing the plan for him and his men was to create a diversion for the main army, not be the primary attack point for it. He knew that by the time he got word to Joab of the possibility, the Ammonites would have shifted the defenses and overwhelmed them. The possibility of him and his men securing two towers was not in the plan and beyond their wildest dream of success. Leaving two men to protect the ladder area for the last of his men to join them, he took his men toward the one tower closest to where the main force would be attacking.

Uriah and his men moved as quietly as they could toward the stone tower with shields held tightly together as if expecting a deadly rain of arrows from the elevated battlements above them, but none came. As they arrived at the heavy wooden door leading into the tower, they were again surprised that it was not only unlocked, but it was left slightly open. Uriah could see a faint light coming from the room beyond the door, perhaps from the trimmed wick of a lantern or the coals of a fire. Either way his eyes were already adjusted to the darkness.

With everything going so smoothly, he expected a trap was waiting for them as he forced the door open and moved quickly into the tower floor room. Instead of a room filled with men waiting with spears and swords to run them through, there were tables and chairs next to the hearth and ten beds with men sleeping quietly in them. At first none of his men moved, then with a nod from Uriah, they moved toward the cots where they covered the mouths of the sleeping men before sending them to their deaths. At the same time, Uriah and another group climbed the ladder leading to the top of the tower. The faint sounds of the muffled screams of dying men could be heard beyond the creaking of the ladder. Uriah knew it was not a warrior's death, nor was there any glory in killing a sleeping man, but they could not risk the chance of a desperate warning cry from a spared life.

With his sword positioned above his head to protect him from the awaiting blows, first Uriah's head, then body cleared the landing, where he was once again met with silence. As he scanned the area, he saw three men along the exterior wall. All three of them were sitting on the floor of the tower and leaning against the outer wall. They had their cloaks wrapped tightly around them and their bows and quivers lying next to them. Two of them were sleeping deeply, while the other, awakened by the creak of the ladder, seemed puzzled at the sight of Uriah climbing to his feet before him. The hesitation was all Uriah needed to close the distance and run his sword through the neck of the guard, turning his attempt to warn his nearby friends into a dying gurgle. He expected the other two to jump to their feet and attack, but the sound of their dying friend was not enough to wake them from their deep sleep. Their lives passed in the same way as the first.

Thinking this would require more of a bloody hand-to-hand attack to secure the tower, Uriah had most of his men bring only swords and shields. The few that he did have bring bows were positioned on the top of the tower to offer support for as long as the arrows they brought and gathered from their enemy were available. Heading back down the ladder, he had the men quietly secure the stairwell hatch that led down to the room below and locked and reinforced the doors that led out to each side of the wall. Once those tasks were completed, he went back up the ladder to the top of the tower and saw that only the faintest light of the sunrise had broken though the darkness and he could now easily make out the enemy towers opposite the one he and his men now held.

Uriah glanced at his men, all of them were beaming with excitement and pride at their success. He returned a brief smile of his own. Although he was proud of them, he was far more relieved that they were all safe and unharmed at this point. Uriah's first impression was that the plan had worked flawlessly, and they had secured the tower and their defensive positions without a single loss. But as he scanned the nearby fortress walls and the two towers at the end of them still held by the enemy, he suddenly realized that their incredible military success had caused the most crucial component of the plan to fail. Instead of the loud, chaotic pitched battle they expected to encounter on the walls, one that would draw hundreds of Ammonite defenders and resources from other wall defenses to their location, there was no movement. Instead of creating a frantic and desperate attempt by the Ammonites to drive him and his men off the wall before the rest of the Israelite army could arrive, they had quietly trapped themselves in a tower without the ability to support it. One of his leaders must have seen the sudden concern on his face.

"What is it?" he asked. Uriah did not respond but continued to feel the growing awareness of the extreme danger that their 'failed successes' had created. With no shifting of defensive forces, Joab would not attack the walls and he and his men would eventually be surrounded and trapped in the tower. His first thought was to order his men out of the tower and back down the ladder, but that would be abandoning the plan. The next thought was to create a loud commotion as planned in hopes it would get the attention of the Ammonites, but an enemy holding a single tower would be of little concern if the wall it protected was not at risk of being overrun. Then another idea crossed his mind that might allow them to create the panic and desperation that they needed from the Ammonites, one he wished he would have acted upon when it first crossed his mind.

"We need to take that other tower," Uriah finally replied and quickly moved to the ladder and back down to where most of his men were waiting. He looked around at the perfect defenses his men had setup and nodded. "Keep that door secured, but I need you to clear a path to the other door," he ordered. Uriah could see the confusion on his men's faces at the order. "We're so good at what we do that we failed to achieve our main goal… to draw the attention and wrath of their whole army on us," he said, hoping the men understood the danger. "We've secured this tower, but without the threat of losing a section of their wall, we are not a big enough threat to the Ammonites. We need to take the other tower," he said. Whether they grasped his explanation or simply were trusting their leader and obeying, they quickly started clearing away the tables and chairs that had been used to reinforce the door.

As some of the men cleared a path to the door, Uriah began selecting the men that would join him in securing the other tower; then he gave defensive orders to those staying. Just as he thought they might be able to recover from the flaw in their plans, a shout was heard from outside the door. Without hesitation, Uriah ordered the door to be opened and he charged through it, taking in what he saw before him in the dim light of dawn. Apparently, a patrol was approaching their tower and as they had been ordered, one of his men above had placed an arrow into the lead member of the patrol, who was now stumbling back in pain and confusion looking for support before falling at the feet of the four remaining soldiers patrolling with him.

At first, the remaining four soldiers stood looking up at the tower in shock, trying to make out in the fading darkness who and why someone had shot one of them, but then seeing the door thrown open violently and Uriah charging out of it toward them, the reality of their situation became clear. The front two tried to recover and lower their spears at Uriah, while the two soldiers behind them turned and fled toward the tower they had just passed through on their patrol, both shouting at the top of their lungs, warning of the imminent danger they had discovered behind them.

Uriah shifted his focus onto the two soldiers in front of him. With the help of surprise and low visibility of the fading dawn, he managed to reach the soldier on his right. His muscle memory from years of training and battle experience allowed him to deflect the tip of the spear with his own sword and then using the momentum of his charge, Uriah thrust it into the soldier's chest. The other soldier was much faster in bringing his spear to bare and thrust it at Uriah's left side. Again, Uriah's experience and training had instinctively directed him to attack the soldier on his right, so that it would keep his shield between him and any attacker on his left. With a quick lift and angle adjustment of his shield, Uriah easily deflected the thrust, causing the tip to pass over his left shoulder, instead of through his chest. That aggressive right-handed attack by the Ammonite left his right side exposed, which Ari, one of Uriah's men who had followed close behind took advantage of and drove his sword into the Ammonites side.

Ignoring the death throes of the two dying soldiers, Uriah was forced to slow his momentum as he struggled to pull his sword from the dying man's chest. Uriah looked up and saw the two remaining soldiers were now running at full speed toward the other tower, shouting warnings with every step they took. Finally wrestling his sword free, he was encouraged to see that several of his men had already leaped past him and were now in close pursuit of the fleeing soldiers.

Uriah, now the follower and not the leader of the attack, tried to survey the situation they faced and build a plan accordingly. Although the other tower was nearly fifty paces away, he felt confident that his men would reach the door before the two fleeing soldiers could enter and close it behind them. But then two things happened that changed that assessment: one, he saw several archers appear on the top of the tower; and two, a soldier, silhouetted by a light behind him, peered through the tower door as if trying to understand the situation before him. Uriah shouted a warning about the archers to his men, but there was nothing he could do about the soldier at the door.

As if all their blessings had run out at the same time, an arrow was released by one of his men in the tower behind him. Whether it was distance or darkness, the arrow missed the soldier at the door, embedding itself in the door next to him. That near miss would prove disastrous to their plans. Instead of holding the door open for his friends to arrive, he slammed it shut on them, leaving their fate to the enemy charging behind them. Seeing that reaching the safety of the tower was no longer an option, the two remaining enemy soldiers spun around and took a defensive stand in front of the now closed door.

With the advantage of speed and stealth now gone, Uriah understood the importance of drawing attention to their battle along the wall. Not only to get the Ammonites to shift their resources, but to let Joab know that it was time for him to unleash the main attack. From the deepest part of his lungs, he released a blood curdling Hittite war cry that few could miss. Understanding the purpose, his men began to shout their own war cries at the Ammonite defenders.

Despite the growing number of arrows raining down on them from above, they quickly eliminated the two remaining soldiers before the door. Although they hoped for a miracle when they reached the door, none was to be found as it was barred and held tight from the other side.

"Ladder wall!" Uriah yelled as he held his shield above his head, keeping it between him and his men, and the archers firing from above. Uriah knew his men understood the command, as it was the very same technique they had planned to use to scale the other tower if the door had been barred. As more of his men arrived, they began assembling as they had practiced. Several held their shields above them to protect those below that were creating a human platform and ladder that would allow them to reach the top of the tower battlements. The support of his own archers firing at the Ammonites from the other tower helped slow the missile fire from above and allowed them the time they needed to safely construct the human ladder. As it reached its desired height, Uriah and several other soldiers sheathed their swords and slid their shields over their shoulders so that they could free their hands for climbing.

As Uriah and his men reached the top of the ladder and within reach of the battlements, he saw that the Ammonites archers had fallen back, and spearmen were moving forward to replace them. As they had practiced and without looking, Uriah reached down and immediately felt a spear shaft meet his hand. To the surprise of the Ammonite spearmen closing on him, in one motion Uriah went from a defenseless target to an armed aggressor pressing the attack from the top of the wall.

Uriah saw that the fellow soldier who had climbed next to him was not so fortunate, and an Ammonite spear had got through before his spear from below could come to bear, but instead of falling back, the soldier held onto the spear embedded in his side, forcing the Ammonite to let go of his weapon and fall back as the additional men who had followed him up the ladder pressed their attack.

Although Uriah's instincts said to try and kill one of the many armed soldiers was gathered in front of him, he knew the best thing he could do was to buy enough time to allow as many of his men as possible to reach the top and join him. With war cries and aggressive lunges, he initially kept the nearest Ammonite soldiers on the defensive and even falling back from his attacks, making more room for his men to join him. First one, then two and finally three of his men had joined him before one of the Ammonites defenders had apparently realized the growing danger. Yelling an order, the once chaotic defenses quickly turned into a formed, almost impregnable, wall of shields and spears that would once again give them the advantage. This would allow them to begin pressing forward their attack and quickly overwhelm Uriah and his few men.

With unsheathed swords in one hand and a spear in the other, Uriah and his men prepared for what he knew was the inevitable. As the Ammonite leader started calling out the shield wall's forward step count, Uriah suddenly saw the Ammonites attention shift from them to something directly behind and above him, their eyes following it to his right. Uriah turned his head slightly, hoping to make out the source of the distraction, and saw that Dathan had reached the top of the battlements, but with no room, decided to use the only path left to him to reach and engage the enemy by running across the top of the wall defenses in an attempt to get behind them.

How Dathan managed to find and keep his footing in the darkness as he leaped between the arrow slit gaps was far less impressive to Uriah than seeing what he did once he made it behind the Ammonites. Without losing momentum, he launched himself directly onto the top of them. The force of Dathan's weight crashing into the side of the tightly packed line of soldiers created the chaos and, more importantly, the opening that Uriah desperately needed.

With the right flank of the Ammonite line now in disarray as they tried to avoid Dathan's spear and regain their balance, Uriah seized the opportunity to slip past the deadly spears that had held him at bay moments before. He drove his spear into the closest defender, pushing him back in the process and allowing Uriah to get past the shield wall spear defenses. Once inside and up close, Uriah knew the long Ammonite spears would be useless in close combat. Yelling and thrusting his sword right, then left in a wild frenzy, Uriah not only dealt death or injury with each thrust of his blade, but he also created the panic and chaos needed in the Ammonite line for his other three men to press their attacks again and creating the additional space they needed for more of his men to reach the top and join them.

At first the Ammonite leader, yelling orders at the top of his lungs, tried to reform the line, but as more of Uriah's men reached the top and slipped through the openings that Uriah and Dathan had created, the line collapsed and the rout and killing began as the Ammonites tried to flee down the passage ladder. This not only left the fleeing Ammonites defenseless, but it also kept any Ammonite reinforcements from coming up the ladder to stop the rout.

As the last of the Ammonite defenders were dispatched, Uriah surveyed the surroundings. Although there were Ammonite dead everywhere, he also saw that several of his men had fallen in the battle as well. Most notably, he saw Dathan sitting on the bloody floor of the tower, an Ammonite spear had passed through his back and was protruding from his chest. From his past battle experience and the placement of the spear, Uriah knew that Dathan's time left on earth would be short. Uriah quickly moved to where he sat and kneeled next to him. Dathan looked up and tried to smile through the pain and labored breath. "Forgot to look behind me," he whispered.

"Yeah, it's kind of hard to do that while flying through the air," Uriah replied, and Dathan fought back the pain and nodded and tried to smile.

"It seemed like a good idea at the time," Dathan slowly and painfully replied, and Uriah reached out to hold Dathan's head in his hands to keep it from falling to the side and he looked intently in Dathan's eyes.

"It was legendary. You saved a lot of men today, my friend," Uriah said confidently, and then watched as the life faded from Dathan's eyes, knowing his soul had left his body. He held him momentarily before laying him on his side. *No time to grieve*, he said to himself and stood back up and looked around.

Uriah let instinct take over and began shouting orders as more and more of his men arrived on top of the wall. "Secure the opening." He shouted, "We don't need any more getting up here until we're ready," he said the last part as if talking to himself. As important as it was to secure the room below, Uriah knew that trying to climb down a ladder where men with long spears waited was suicide for the few remaining men he had available.

Uriah quickly moved to look down from the edge of the battlements and saw scores of Ammonite soldiers charging across the wall from the other tower. "I need some archers over here. If you don't have a bow, use the ones the Ammonites gave us." He pointed to the dead Ammonite archers scattered across the floor of the tower. He then moved to survey the tower the rest of his men were defending, then at the four men below who had formed the bottom of the ladder and now could not reach the top to join them.

Knowing the lower tower door opened outwards, not inwards, Uriah shouted down to them. "Spike and hold that door closed for as long as you can. Don't let them out or we'll lose the wall," he shouted and watched as they began pounding their daggers into the edges of the door frame, and using their spears to brace the door closed by thrusting the tip of the spear into the wooden door and the base of the spear against the edge of one of the floor stones.

He had 15 men holding the original tower, 15 at the top of this tower, 4 holding the door below and 6 men that either were dead or could no longer hold a sword or spear in a fight. The good news was that shouts and alarms could now be heard across the city.

As the last of his defensive orders were finalized, Uriah glanced briefly at the distant hill where he knew Joab was watching, as if signaling that it was time for him to hold up his end of this deadly plan. He and his men had achieved even more than he had promised and if they could hold this section of the wall, it would give Joab another clear option for taking the city. He just hoped Joab would realize it in time.

Chapter 16
The perfect plan
(Joab)

With Joab's main army out of sight from the Ammonite city walls, they waited patiently and eagerly to receive the attack order from Joab at just the right time. It was an order that Joab had no intention of giving today. From a vantage point on a nearby hill and with his brother Abishai standing next to him, Joab waited and watched through the fading darkness for his plan to unfold. He was waiting not only for Uriah's attack to begin, but to see how quickly his deadly plan would unfold to the demise of Uriah and his men. *No, David's plan*, Joab reminded himself. *Soon Uriah, or you will lose the darkness.* he stated softly as if reminding Uriah of his need to attack.

Had Uriah had a change of heart? Did he realize or discover the real plan? Joab wondered as the unanticipated delay continued. Suddenly, a younger soldier with far better eyesight than his own began relaying what he was seeing to Joab. "It has begun. The ladder is up, and they are climbing it," he said, then halted his narration. Joab was having difficulty making out the figures and scene he knew the soldier was describing but kept staring in that direction anyway.

He was confident that Uriah would be at the lead, and Joab hoped to hear the immediate sound of battle and shouts of warning coming from the Ammonites at their discovery of Uriah and his men on their walls, a discovery that would halt the attack and leave Uriah trapped and killed on the upper wall. Joab wished for an early discovery, not just because it would bring the plan to an end, but it would also save most of Uriah's men from the same fate, forcing them to withdraw.

"They appear to have secured the top of the wall and are moving toward the southern tower as planned," the young soldier said with excitement and those around him, including his brother, quietly cheered the efforts to Joab's frustration.

"Good," Joab replied, more for appearance's sake than personal joy, and waited for the next update and sounds of battle. When the observing soldier had not reported for several moments, Joab cleared his throat as a reminder of his job. "Sorry, sir. It appears they have taken the inside and top of the tower without raising an alarm!" he said in excitement and disbelief. Joab's heart sank as he realized the most important part of his plan, Uriah's attack being discovered early, had failed. His mind raced as he knew his runners and signalers were waiting for him to give the order to launch the attack, an order he had never planned to give at any point in time.

"Sir?" one of his leaders stated as if reminding Joab of his commitment to Uriah and his men. Then the reason for not giving the order finally came to him.

"Hold. The Ammonites have not shifted their defenses to retake the tower," he said and then tried to think of what his next action, or more accurately excuse, he was going to use once the Ammonites did react. Joab knew that with darkness fading quickly, his plan of keeping Uriah's situation hidden from the other army's sight, along with any decisions he made in not ordering the attack that would save Uriah, were fading as well. If the army could see Uriah's success, and the movement of defenders toward him and his men, then he would have a difficult time justifying his withholding of the attack order.

"Sir, I think they are withdrawing from the tower," the sharp-eyed soldier reported with a confused tone. Joab surmised that Uriah had come to the same conclusion he had and was trying to save his men before they became trapped in the tower. Joab's gut knotted at the thought of his plan failing after all this careful planning. He also hated the thought of instead of Uriah's death, there would be discussions of his victory and bravery of taking the tower without loss. It would become the topic of discussion and songs around the fires at night. Just as he was about to give the order for the main army to stand down, the soldier added to his report. "Sir, they aren't abandoning the tower. They are trying to take the other one too!" He said with an increased level of excitement and pride.

Joab stepped forward as if thinking those two steps would suddenly make it easier for him to make out the distant towers and what was unfolding there. *What are you doing Uriah?* He asked himself as he tried to grasp the reason for taking the tower. It was his brother that provided the answer.

"If Uriah manages to take that tower, it will give us the protected pathway we need into the city," he said excitedly. Joab nodded in agreement, but he was still more concerned with ensuring that his original plan would work, than the opportunity of taking the city.

"They have been discovered and there is fighting along the top of the wall leading to the tower," the soldier stated more calmly than before, and Joab began hearing the growing sound of battle cries and shouts of warning. "They are trying to reach the top of the tower," the soldier reported nervously. Joab knew that meant the tower door was barred from the inside and almost impregnable without the right tools to force it open, tools he knew Uriah and his men did not have.

"What is your plan should he take it?" Abishai asked quietly, as if making sure his brother was prepared to give the necessary orders. Abishai had always been a man of action, often sudden actions that would get them both into trouble. On the other hand, his own need to carefully think things through before acting had led to missed opportunities as well. A calming reality of Uriah's situation came to mind.

"He barely had enough men to take and hold one tower, let alone two. By the time we shift forces to help, the towers will have been lost and our troops exposed," he said quietly, still thinking through the multitude of options unfolding before him and the excuses he would need to create with each potential one. "Perhaps he will create the diversion we needed, where he failed before," Joab replied. He could tell by the response from his brother and the men around him that he should not have used 'failed' to describe Uriah's efforts, but he could think of nothing to say that would remedy it.

Joab could finally see in the growing light the ladder wall of men that had formed at the base of the tower. As before, he was confident that if Uriah still lived, he would be the lead soldier climbing the ladder to reach and engage the waiting defenders. Joab saw that two or three additional men were following closely behind the first. *What if he took the tower?* He wondered nervously, and then saw the flow of men trying to reach the top stop. It appeared Uriah's bravery and good fortune had finally run out. However, just as that thought ended, he saw that another soldier had managed to climb upon the outer wall battlements. The soldier then leaped his way along the top of the outer wall of the tower before launching himself into the battle from another point of attack. A few grunts and cheers went up from those standing by Joab at the aggressive maneuver made by the soldier. Moments later, the flow of men reaching the top continued until there was not enough to form the ladder. Joab realized, as did the rest of those with him, that Uriah had taken the tower.

"Perhaps we could send some of our reserves to help him hold those towers?" Abishai finally suggested as if prompting his brother to act. As much as he wanted to see his plan succeed, it was becoming harder to ignore the opportunity before him. Looking down at the field before the wall of the city, he saw soldiers were crossing it at full speed toward Uriah's newly claimed wall.

"It appears someone has already given that order without my consent," Joab said coldly. Those standing nearby recognized the leadership mistake that had been made by making such an important decision without seeking Joab's direction first.

"Should we order the main army to relocate and support Uriah's section?" Abishai asked his brother and waited. Joab tried to conceal the anger that was evident to all. Although those nearby thought his anger was a result of men acting without his orders, the true reason was far deeper and selfish. It was bad enough that his careful plan had been foiled by Uriah's success, but the idea of Uriah getting the credit for the taking of the city burned in his craw. Joab shook his head.

"It's best that we stay with the plan," Joab said curtly and turned to look directly at his brother. "When the Ammonites begin shifting their forces to stop the breach, then the original wall will be vulnerable for taking. That is our plan and that is what we will do," Joab stated strongly as if giving an order, then turned back to observe the battlements.

Joab could see in the growing light that more and more Ammonite defenders across the battlements were now awake from their slumber and taking their defensive positions as they were trained to do. He also knew that their leaders would be trying to ascertain how best to respond to the Israelite attack unfolding before them. What started as a trickle, became a growing flow of soldiers moving to reinforce the section of the wall that had apparently fallen to the enemy.

In the growing light of morning, they first saw small groups of Ammonite soldiers probe the defenses of the two fallen towers from both sides, each failing to reclaim them. Joab saw that the number of soldiers that had been ordered to reinforce Uriah's breach was far less than he anticipated, perhaps 10 soldiers at most had climbed the original wall ladder to reach the battlements. With so few soldiers, perhaps Uriah would not be able to hold the two towers after all.

Joab, along with every other leader standing there with him, knew that without committing his full army of troops to the breach that two things would happen: one, the two towers Uriah held would fall; two, the Ammonites would start to realize that this attack was only a feint to draw them in. Joab wrestled with the decision, knowing the longer he delayed it, the more time it would give the Ammonites to help his original plan to succeed.

"What are your orders?" Abishai suddenly broke the silence, knowing full well the importance of the orders that Joab would give in the next few moments. Joab could see that the Ammonites were now waiting as well for what the commander of the Israel army would do.

"If we relocate our army, the Ammonites will throw everything they have to retake those two towers and block our attack. If we don't, they will shift them back to defend the other sections of the wall and deal with the breach later," Joab stated out loud what everyone was thinking.

"If we do nothing, Uriah and his men will be defeated," one of his advisors quietly mumbled, pointing out the obvious cost of their inaction. Joab turned and glared at him.

"Do you think I don't know that!" Joab shot back. "Do you think the Ammonites don't know that as well?" he shouted louder than before for effect. "It is clear the plan has failed, so how many men should we now risk losing for the slim chance that we can save Uriah and his men? Hundreds, perhaps thousands," Joab replied and glanced around the room.

"At least order the army to shift and prepare to attack the breach. I will gather as many men as I can from here and reinforce Uriah's position. If we can hold the towers long enough for the army to arrive, then the wall and city will be ours!" Abishai asked, almost begging Joab for permission.

"The Ammonites are mounting another attack on the southern tower," the soldier reported, and they turned to watch as Ammonite soldiers began pouring out of the nearby tower, carrying ladders above their heads.

"Brother?" Abishai asked in an almost demanding voice, trying to get Joab to give the order to send him to help. Joab watched as the ladders reached the base of the tower and then tipped upwards toward the battlements. Soldiers began to flow up the ladders and were met by Uriah's men. Joab shook his head.

"It is too late. I will not send any more men to their deaths," Joab stated firmly.

Abishai stepped over close to Joab and tried to speak his words as quietly as he could. "There is chance for your plan to succeed, but we…" Joab cut him off before he could finish and stared at him with a look and hidden message that only two brothers could understand.

"This was David's plan, not mine," he told him firmly, holding his gaze long enough to make sure he understood there was more to his answer than what he was saying out loud.

Abishai was at first angry with the interruption, then confused, as he tried to grasp his brother's hidden meaning. As it came to him, he at first tried to dismiss it, but the subtle nod from Joab, sent a chill rushing through his heart. He tried to find words that would somehow support his brothers actions and orders to those listening nearby, but he was speechless and all he could do was nod.

Chapter 17
A betrayed trust
(Uriah)

After he and his men had driven off the most recent assault from the Ammonites attempt to reclaim their tower, Uriah took a moment to bandage a wound from an arrow that had passed through his upper leg. As he was wrapping that wound, he noticed he had several other wounds on his arms and shoulders that were bleeding as well. Knowing he had far more pressing matters to deal with, he decided those wounds could wait.

He quickly surveyed the condition of his men and their defenses. Of the 16 men that had reached the top of the tower with him, only 7 remained that were able to still hold a sword or bow. They had stacked the bodies of the dead Ammonites on top of an overturned bench they had placed over the floor entrance to the tower from below. He felt confident that the wood and weight of the bodies was preventing any attacks from that area, at least for the foreseeable future. He watched as several of his men were moving about, gathering any arrows in the area that they could find to help replenish their empty quivers. Staying low to avoid the growing number of arrows coming from the other tower, they gathered what was available on the ground and even pulled them from the bodies of both Ammonite and Israelite soldiers.

"Joab's sending the army!" one of his men shouted and pointed over the tower battlements. Staying low, Uriah rushed to the edge of the wall and quickly glanced down at the now dawn lit area of the wall that they had climbed earlier in the darkness. During the short glance before ducking back down, he was expecting to see thousands of soldiers pouring up and over the walls to help secure their victory, but instead, he saw what appeared to be only a few men climbing the lone ladder. He moved to a better vantage point that would enable him to see the wall between their two towers. As he glanced down again, what he saw filled his heart with a mix of emotions. Instead of a vast number of reinforcements, there were only 10 brave men coming to their aid. He knew they were the 10 men he held back from the attack that had strongly doubted the plan and Uriah's decision to accept it.

Uriah slid back down behind the protection of the battlements and tried to hold back his emotions. Tears welled up in his eyes at how proud he was in his men, not just the ones he had wrongly agreed to take into battle, but even the 10 that had now apparently forfeited their lives to be with him. They lived as a family and apparently now they would die together as one.

Uriah cleared his mind and tried to understand what the arrival of these ten men meant from a broader understanding. With the growing number of Ammonite soldiers being used with each attack to reclaim the towers, Uriah new that the addition of just ten men would do little to hold them back, perhaps just delay the inevitable a few minutes longer. He glanced again toward the hill where he knew Joab was watching and the open fields where the army would be moving across if the order had been given. Not only were there no additional soldiers that could be seen, but he could also see no dust in the distance that would indicate the army was coming. They were alone.

Uriah closed his eyes and tried to replay all that had happened in the past week. He had been invited to eat and spend time with the King, he had chosen to miss an opportunity to spend one last precious moment with his wife, and then was asked by the King to have him and his men be the lead in a very dangerous plan. He knew full well that not all pride was bad, but when it clouds our judgement or causes us to ignore common sense to please someone else, then pride can kill. Sometimes it kills just you, sometimes it can wound or kill all those around you. The very ones you love more than even the King.

He thought of Bathsheba, her smile, her lips, her curves and her laughter. He had been so busy winning wars for the King that he had left her with no heir to take care of her, or to remember him by. Had he just listened to David and gone home one of those two evenings in Jerusalem, he wondered if things could have been different. He thought of the families of all his men and the loss that they would all share together as they grieved over their husbands, fathers, and sons. Would their sons and daughters grow bitter toward God at their loss, a loss that could have been prevented if it were not for his pride and selfish ambition?

And David - would the King grieve over the loss of him and his men, or would they just be another statistic in a growing list of the dead that had served faithfully under his rule? Uriah suddenly realized that he now cared little as to what the King thought, the only thing that truly mattered was the impact this would have on the families of him and his men, and more importantly, what God would say. The latter thought on God seemed to linger in his thoughts. Although his knowledge of the God of the Israelites was limited, he had learned and seen enough of His power and glory to know that pleasing him had far more eternal consequences and blessings than pleasing the King. God and family was priority, honoring an earthly king a distant second. Although it seemed a little late to realize and grasp something so important, he at least felt at peace with the now clear understanding as he embraced it.

Rising above the sound of a battering ram hitting the braced door along the wall his men held below them, there was suddenly a grunting and scaping sound of men climbing the walls above it. The sound brought Uriah out of his deep thoughts, and he looked toward the noise to see first one, then four more familiar faces of his men climb up and over the battlements. Despite having arrows embedded in their shields and some even in their bodies, each had managed to carry over the walls with them a bundle of arrows on their backs and sacks of extra food and water. Although he was happy to see them and the supplies they brought with them, he was saddened with the understanding of their decision.

"I thought I ordered you to stay back?" Uriah grumbled at the five men who had joined them, each moving to take defensive positions along the wall. Emmet crawled toward where Uriah was sitting. Emmet glanced around, taking in the situation as he responded.

"Well, the biblical requirement of having to marry and take care of all your wives and children seemed rather daunting at my age," he replied and patted Uriah on the shoulder. Uriah tried to smile at the comment, but his thoughts turned serious again.

"Joab's not coming is he," Uriah stated more as a fact than a question, which Emmet confirmed by shaking his head. "How are the men by the door holding up?" Uriah asked, knowing that Emmet had just passed them.

"The door is starting to buckle, and the Ammonites are shifting their archers to the rooftops of the nearby buildings behind the walls and on the ground below. We all paid a heavy price getting here," he said, and Uriah could see blood coming from the broken shaft of an arrow in Emmet's hip. "Any chance of talking you into climbing back down and off this wall?" Emmet asked. Uriah looked at his men and knew that most would not be able to climb down due to their wounds. He knew what the Ammonites would do to them if they left them behind. He shook his head. "I thought that was what you were going to say," Emmet replied.

"I should have listened to you and the others. I'm sorry," Uriah said, and Emmet held his gaze a moment, then smiled and nodded.

"I'm sorry for not being more adamant about opposing you," he replied with a faint chuckle and reached out his hand. "Forgiven?" Emmet asked and Uriah nodded and grasped his arm.

"Here they come again," Aviv shouted from where he was observing the defenses facing the Ammonite tower, then quickly rose and fired an arrow into the approaching attackers. Helping each other up, Emmet moved toward the area under attack while Uriah looked down the wall at his men doing their best to hold the tower door below. Seeing their doomed situation, he shouted an order down at them.

"Either go and convince Joab to send more men, or head to the other tower and help them!" he yelled, hoping that they would choose the first part of his order and save themselves, but somehow knowing they would choose the tower. Even as brief as the moment was, arrows from the Ammonites began ricocheting off the area of wall where he had just been. He knew that with the growing number of Ammonite archers firing from the city and below, that they would be hard pressed to reach either. He also knew that once the door below was breached, they would also have to defend against attacks from this side of the tower as well. He grasped the fact that when the door was breached the same fate awaited his men in the other tower.

Uriah limped to the opposite side to join his men as they prepared for the next attack. He glanced briefly at the number and formation of the Ammonite attackers and knew that the Ammonites had fully committed to this attack. They had finally organized an effective shield wall in front that would also protect their soldiers marching behind them, they had ladders prepared and ready to reach the upper areas, and they had gathered the number of soldiers they needed to press the attack for as long as needed to achieve victory. Uriah could see that there were even more soldiers still pouring out the door of the distant tower to support them.

Uriah and his men understood that even if Joab had a change of heart and decided to send help, the reinforcements would not arrive in time to save them. The finality of the situation hit them all and they glanced back and forth at each other as if confirming it and saying their short goodbyes with a nod. They stayed low to avoid the arrows and waited for the enemy soldiers to come within reach of their swords and spears. It was not but a moment later that they heard the sound of steps and grunts from the ladders being climbed.

"These uncircumcised Ammonites have been harassing and killing our families for decades. So, let's make sure we take as many of them with us as possible!" Uriah yelled and then ran his spear through the helmet of the first Ammonite that reached the top, then they all yelled their battle cries and moved forward to engage the additional soldiers reaching the top of the wall. The cries were not only to send fear into the Ammonites, but to remind the men watching from the nearby hill that they were warriors to the end. Beginning with their spears, they lunged at the attackers, striking and slashing with such frenzy and reckless abandon that blood began to cover the outer wall of the tower.

Chapter 18
Bloodguilt and justification
(Joab)

Of all the things Joab expected from the leaders when they learned of Uriah and his men's death at the hands of the Ammonites, silence was not one of them. Even his own brother did not want to speak with him of the failed plan and the battle they had witnessed atop the walls of the Ammonite city. He had prepared a hundred responses to what he thought would be the hundred questions that he expected them to ask in anger, but there was nothing but silence toward him. He could hear them quietly discussing what had happened between themselves and those that witnessed it. Although Joab could see that Abishai was involved in most of those discussions, he was never included.

As the silence grew, his thoughts shifted from how he would explain his actions, to far more sinister questions and concerns. Were they discussing his leadership abilities? Were they plotting to remove him as the general of the army? Had someone learned of the truth of the failed attack? Had David set him up to take the fall for Uriah's death? Who was his greatest threat in the leadership group should they decide to try and remove him? Had his own brother betrayed him? Finally, how far was he willing to go to prevent such a coup? He felt that he needed to quickly rein in all the plotting and planning that was happening behind his back before those behind it could act.

Joab had called a meeting of his leaders and as they filed one by one into the meeting tent, he tried to use all his talents and abilities to read their expressions to discover who was behind such plans. If there was a usurper amongst them, their faces did not reveal it. Sitting in their leadership circle, he sat in the traditional position of leader and continued to scan the room. Few would look up at him, let alone meet his eyes. Would they try to kill him during the meeting?

Would his brother, who was sitting close by, try to stop such an attack? His heart raced and nervous sweat trickled down his back as he looked at all the swords and daggers hanging from belts or sitting on the laps of these leaders. Whenever it came, he knew it would be over quickly.

It was Amos, one of the younger leaders sitting closest to him, who was the first to move. Rising from a sitting position to his knees, he shifted his sword to his right hand and finally looked up at Joab. *So, you are my betrayer,* Joab thought as he waited for the attack.

"Your brother has shared with us what took place with Uriah and his men and your decision to withhold sending the army," Amos began, and Joab's heart sank to learn that his brother was behind the plot to overthrow him. "I, we, cannot imagine the sorrow and pain you must be experiencing at the loss of Uriah and his men, while you could do nothing to save them." Joab's heart skipped a beat in confusion at Amos's words of kindness and compassion, not in accusation or condemnation. Joab realized that their silence and quiet discussions were not venting their anger toward him, or plotting his demise, but shielding him from what they felt was his pain and the guilt of it. A sense of relief washed over him as he tried to recover his thoughts and the shift from the fear to gratitude toward his leaders. He glanced briefly at his brother, realizing that he had not been plotting against him, but was working hard to refine and change the narrative of what was being told that would help portray Joab, and the decisions had made, in a far better light than what unfolded.

"Thank you, Amos. It has been heavy on my heart," he replied, knowing it was a lie and tried to think of additional words to support his statement and ease their concerns. "I have replayed those moments over and over in my mind, somehow trying to find where I could have saved them," he said and shook his head, allowing the new understanding and reason for their silence to open new pathway discussions. "I hope you can find it in your hearts to forgive the failure in finding a way to save them. I know the King will be disappointed to learn that despite our best efforts, his plan had failed at the cost of so many," he ended, making sure most of the blame would fall on someone else. "I should have more adamantly shared my opposition to the plan, but to my shame, instead I did my best to support it. Please forgive me," he ended and bowed his head.

There was considerable mumbling coming from various leaders in the room, but it was followed by the nodding of heads. It was Amos who spoke first again. "I felt the same apprehension, and I did not speak up either. I also ask the forgiveness of those gathered here," he said, and they mumbled and nodded in response. Several more spoke up and shared the same, asking for the group's forgiveness as well.

Although Joab smiled humbly as the leaders asked for forgiveness, his smile was about how he had managed to shift blame and responsibility that once rested solely on him, to everyone in the room.

"Brothers, I value and need your counsel. Let us agree to never hold back when insights or wisdom prompts us." He looked down the rows of men, making eye contact with each one until each responded in agreement with either their voice or with a nod of their head. "From this day forward, let the memory and bravery of Uriah and his men be a reminder of this commitment and vow to one another," Joab stated and those gathered nodded in agreement.

With the crisis averted, Joab brought the meeting to an end. Joab thought of one more way to, not only distance himself from the Uriah matter, but strengthen the new loyalty opportunity with another. As the leaders were beginning to file out, he asked Amos if he would stay a moment longer to discuss an important matter. Once everyone had left, Amos stood quietly in the center of the room and waited.

Joab poured wine into two cups, giving one to Amos and then raised his cup. "To Uriah and his men and may another take his place," Joab toasted, and Amos nodded and drank with him.

Joab let the silence grow as he seemed to take his time swallowing the wine, then cleared his throat. "Amos, Uriah was very valuable and loyal to the King and to me. I need someone who is just as capable and loyal to take his place in my leadership council." Joab let the moment sink in before continuing. "I believe you are that man; however, my question is, do you believe you are?" Joab tried to read Amos's expression as he contemplated the question. Joab could see that his body language began to change and he started nodding with pride.

"I do, and thank you for that belief in me," Amos replied proudly.

"I want you to deliver an important message to King David in Jerusalem. I need someone I can trust to explain the loss of Uriah and his men accurately," Joab asked, and Amos nodded in agreement, yet with apprehension.[1]

"I will send a full account of the battle, but when you have finished giving the king this account of battle, the king's anger may flare up, and he may ask you, 'Why did you get so close to the city to fight? Didn't you know they would shoot arrows from the wall? Who killed Abimelek son of Jerub-Besheth? Didn't a woman drop an upper millstone from the wall, so that he died in Thebez? Why did you get so close to the wall?' If he asks you this, then say to him, 'Moreover, your servant Uriah the Hittite, is dead,'" Joab then handed Amos his account of battle for him to read to the king.

As Amos began reading the letter, Joab watched his expression change several times before he finished and looked up at Joab as if trying to understand.

"I know it's not exactly as it happened, but I do not want David to feel the bloodguilt of Uriah's loss because the plan the king provided us failed." Joab paused and watched as Amos tried to grasp the meaning of his words. "You will learn that it is often best if we take the blame for those we follow. It is my duty to spare the king from such shame by taking the blame for this failure," Joab said in a humble tone. Amos at first seemed shocked by Joab's willingness to sacrifice his reputation and honor for David, but then seemed to understand and nodded.

"I understand and will do as you ask and report this as stated. Thank you again for this honor," Amos replied and bowed his head slightly to Joab.

"I will need you to depart at your earliest opportunity, today if possible. I do not want David to hear what happened from anyone else," he stated, and Amos nodded in agreement and left. Although Joab could see that by giving Amos this honor, he had won the loyalty of a young man to his team, more importantly he had taught him the true cost of such loyalty and the need to protect his leader from the blame of future mistakes, just as Joab was doing for David. Joab knew that the longer he was in power, the more loyal young men he would need to 'fall on their swords' for him when needed or asked, to cover his mistakes.

As Amos left the meeting tent, Abishai quietly entered and walked over and poured himself a cup of wine, then turned and stared at Joab while he drank it before finally setting the cup down. "The guilty flee, though no one pursues them," Joab's brother quoted the well-known proverb and smiled. "I could tell you were spending more time thinking about your worst fears happening, instead of taking the action needed to prevent them," Abishai said with a smile.

"I owe you a great deal brother. You know me too well and yes, that turned out far different from what I had expected," Joab said and held up his cup to his brother. Abishai poured himself another cup of wine, acknowledged his brother and drank it.

"Now that that is behind us, do you mind telling me why David wanted Uriah dead? Or was his death your idea and I just missed your meaning?" Abishai asked bluntly. Joab knew that his brother's directness was his greatest strength, but also what bothered him the most when they were growing up together. Joab pondered his question before replying.

"I have no idea. He never explained the reason, he just sent me a note telling me to send Uriah into battle where he would be killed," Joab said. "I thought he was one of David's most loyal and capable men. Why he would want him dead…" Joab paused and shrugged his shoulders, "I honestly would never have thought David was capable of such actions." Abishai seemed to be deep in thought as he stood up and headed toward the entrance of the tent. "Where are you going?" Joab asked, and Abishai turned and smiled.

"Sounds like I need to go with Amos to see what I can learn in Jerusalem," Abishai replied.

"Can you at least try to be subtle?" Joab asked and his brother smiled.

"I'm always subtle," Abishai replied, pretending he was shocked by the request. Joab shook his head and took a deep breath. It had been a busy day, but it ended well. He thought about Amos and ways he could pull him tighter into his leadership circle. Then in the quiet of the moment, his mind drifted back to earlier in the morning, and the battle that he watched play out on the distant wall, the bravery of Uriah and his men as they met the Ammonites pouring over the walls. For several minutes they held back the attackers, inflicting such terrible losses on them that Joab feared they would continue to hold the towers. However, time and numbers were always in the Ammonites favor, and Joab knew Uriah and his men had fought as one and died as one on that wall.

As the moments passed by, he coldly replaced the thoughts of the loss of Uriah and his men with the thoughts of the group of leaders. More specifically, he considered who in that group of men he could begin to groom, those who would be willing to shield him from blame, keep him in power and help him remain the leader of the army of Israel. Perhaps even king someday.

[1] 2 Samuel 11:19-25

Chapter 19
Seeds of doubt
(Nathan)

As was often the custom, a custom David established within his leadership, a priest of God was asked to sit with the King as counsel during days when the people would bring their grievances and requests to the King. The issues stemming from disagreements between two parties which could not be mediated by officials would be referred to the king, trusting in David and his advisors to render the final and fair decision on the matter.[1]

For the most part, Nathan did not mind hearing the people from both sides present their cases to the King. Some were very articulate and detailed, others simply an outpouring of emotion and hurt that had less to do with finding a solution or rendering a decision than the need to be heard by someone of authority. The detailed cases were much easier to find a path or solution that could mend both sides of the relationship at stake, something Nathan enjoyed helping David navigate the facts to find the solution. Whereas finding a solution for the more emotion-based cases was far more difficult to navigate. Over time, Nathan came to realize that most of these cases came from people who had been hurt by either their own poor choices and were in denial, or they were simply looking for mercy when none was given by the opposing party.

However, what truly interested Nathan were the cases where people were truly taken advantage of by people of power or position, and without access to the King, they would have no one of greater power who could overturn such abuse and hold the abusers accountable. Like Nathan, David always had a heart and more of an interest in such cases and had a long history of rendering severe punishment and consequences when such abusers were brought before him. Nathan also knew that it was the possibility of such severe consequences being assessed by David that kept such abusers in check.

Even with the possibility of such consequences, Nathan learned that many such cases never made it to David. Threats, intimidation, character assassinations, shaming and even the collusion and involvement of other leadership authorities or people of power, were powerful and effective tools of the abusers, tools whose sole purpose was to crush an opponent's pursuit of justice long before it could reach the king.

Nathan had personally championed such cases, some when they were either brought to him at the temple by someone who had been broken and crushed by such abusers, or God had revealed a situation to him personally. Although at first naïve about the issues, he gradually learned that this abuse of power could be found working its way into every level of society and that it was a learned and then imitated technique. It was generally repeated after it was first used effectively by business leaders, government authorities, soldiers of rank, and even by priestly members within the temple. It was an evil practice that, if it not dealt with quickly and severely, would work its way through all aspects of leadership and society. Nathan was grateful that David did not condone such abuse of power and was willing to listen to grievances of those nature and to insure justice was done.

It was during such a case, as David was strongly rebuking a government official for such abuse, that Nathan saw Amos, one of David's military leaders, step into the back part of the room. It caught his eye only because rarely did he see military leaders involved in such cases, unless they were the ones being brought before David. In a final judgement, Nathan listened as David not only removed a government official from a position of power, but he also required him to personally pay full restitution to the abused and provide a detailed list of the names of all those involved. Nathan understood that David not only wanted to remove the bad fruit from the leadership tree but, if necessary, to pull it out from the roots.

David must have also noticed Amos waiting in the back of the room and signaled for a break in the presentation of cases to the King. As the remaining people were guided to the exits and the door was shut, David motioned for Amos to come forward.

"It is good to see you Amos, what brings you to Jerusalem?" David asked and watched as Amos stepped forward with a sealed scroll and handed it to David.

"Thank you, my King. I bring news from Commander Joab at Rabbah," Amos replied, while David broke the seal and started reading the contents within the letter. At first Nathan watched as David's face turned from interest to anger, shaking his head as he finished, crushing the letter he held. David eventually looked up at the messenger as if trying to understand.

"The men overpowered us and came out against us in the open, but we drove them back to the entrance of the city gate. Then the archers shot arrows at your servants from the wall, and some of the king's men died. Moreover, your servant Uriah the Hittite is dead," Amos confirmed the story that he knew Joab had shared in the letter, the one he practiced, and repeated directly to David, only this time, he included the additional explanation that Joab had told him to do about the death of Uriah and his men.

At hearing the news of Uriah's death, Nathan's heart sank with sorrow, and he immediately thought of Uriah's wife Bathsheba and his household. Expecting the same, if not greater, hurt and mourning from David, Nathan was shocked at his composure.

"Say this to Joab when you return: 'Don't let this upset you; the sword devours one as well as another. Press the attack against the city and destroy it.'" David replied calmly and leaned back in his chair. Nathan waited for David to inquire more deeply as to what happened, who else was lost in the battle, but instead he seemed in deep thought, perhaps too distraught to ask. So, Nathan took it upon himself to inquire as David recovered.

"And what of Uriah's men, how are they taking his death?" Nathan asked. Amos averted his eyes and seemed to have difficulty finding the words before finally answering the question.

"They were with Uriah and were also lost in the battle," Amos replied softly. Nathan's heart fell at the news, and he looked at David, expecting a similar response, but David remained silent as if lost in thought.

"Are you saying all of them were killed?" Nathan asked in shock and watched as Amos nodded his head without looking up. Nathan stood up and walked to the balcony window, trying to gather his emotions. Less than a week ago he had personally met and delivered messages to each of their family members. Now they were all dead, killed in battle. *How can this be Lord?* Nathan silently cried out to the Lord from his heart, filled with pain and sorrow for the men and their families. Then he thought of David and his quiet response. What inner pain and sorrow he must also be feeling, losing such a great leader and the men Uriah had trained and mentored. Nathan considered it was his responsibility to counsel and even console the king when needed; yet instead, he was outside mourning alone. Once he felt he had gathered his emotions, Nathan walked back into the room to fulfill his responsibilities.

As he quietly reentered the room, he looked around and saw that Amos was no longer there. In fact, everyone had been dismissed and only David remained in the room still sitting in his leadership chair. As Nathan came around from behind the chair, he was not sure what to expect, but he was prepared to console or counsel, whatever his David's needs might be. David seemed startled to see him when he came into view, apparently not knowing that he had walked out onto the balcony earlier. Nathan was expecting to see tears, or at least deep sadness in David's face, but there was none behind the startled face. Nathan realized that David had seen battles and death many times and knew how to numb his emotions when such reports arrive. They both seemed at a loss for words. Nathan was waiting for an order or command to come from his king, while David seemed to be expecting the some direction to come from the prophet. Nathan was the first to break the awkward silence.

"My king, would you allow me to personally deliver the news to the families of Uriah and his men?" Nathan asked. "This will allow the families to begin shiva, the week of mourning," David seemed relieved by Nathan's suggestion and nodded, then exhaled and seemed to gather his thoughts again.

"I will deliver the news to Uriah's wife," David said. "It's the least I can do." Based on the last time he encountered Bathsheba and her servant, Nathan was at first relieved at David's decision, but then had a change of heart.

"My king, I believe it might be best if the news comes from a man of God who can offer spiritual support and prayer when they hear the news. Perhaps you could write a personal letter that I can deliver to all the families on your behalf," Nathan suggested. At first, David seemed upset at the suggestion but then relented and nodded.

"I will have them written and signed for you to deliver today," David finally replied and turned away. Nathan had learned that was a signal that their time together was over. He bowed and began walking toward the door, then stopped and turned back to face the king.

"Do you want to talk about the loss of Uriah and his men?" Nathan asked. David at first seemed nervous at the question when looked at Nathan, but then shook his head.

"No. Thank you for the offer," David replied with a smile. Nathan thought of pushing the idea of helping David deal with the grief of the loss but felt perhaps a later time would be better.

"I have their names if you need them," Nathan stated and paused by the door as he waited for David's reply, but he seemed confused by the question. "The names of the soldiers and family members. I have them if you need them," Nathan stated, and David seemed to grasp the meaning and nodded.

"That would be helpful. Please give the names to my assistant as you leave," David said, and then turned and walked toward the balcony.

Nathan stood on the other side of the door trying to understand David's emotional and physical response. Having the incredible blessing of being David's trusted counsel and spiritual advisor for the past years, Nathan had seen him at both his worst and best in his faith. However, during the past month he had not seen him respond to such news like he did today. Either he was in deep mourning that Nathan had never witnessed before, or there was something far different going on inside that David was unwilling to share.

Nathan shifted his thoughts from David to himself and thought about how different these fifty visits to the families of Uriah's men would be than the last one. His last visit brought joy and happiness; this would be the opposite. Nathan was not a trained warrior, but he had sat in counsel many times with David and his leaders. The question that seemed to circle back into his mind was how, not just Uriah but all his men had died in that one encounter with the Ammonites in front of the wall, no soldier from another unit, just his. What also was odd was how David had replied to the news, not the endless string of questions he would normally ask about the encounter when even a single soldier had perished. Today he learned he lost fifty men, including one of his best leaders, and he only asked Amos one question about the battle.

Nathan wondered if the dreams he had been having about David the past month had made him over sensitive, and the dreams were influencing how he was perceiving and reacting to news and events relating to David. Usually, such dreams were meant as a warning or as an encouragement from God, but Nathan had been unable to understand, let alone interpret, any of them. Prayer and fasting had not helped clarify them either, so what was he missing?

Why God had put it on his heart to remember each family name of Uriah's men seemed odd at the time, but it was clear to Nathan now. God knew what was coming and even preparing him for such a task. Even David's assistant seemed surprised by his ability to list all of them from memory as he prepared each of the sheets of parchment for David to write. Nathan knew each letter David would write would not be long in words or explanations, but a simple condolence statement signed by the king. Although a sheet of parchment had little value, because the words came from the king, he knew the family would treasure it more than from anyone else. *How strange is the power of kings,* Nathan thought as he waited for the letters to be written so that he could deliver them.

[1] 1 Chronicles 18:14-15

Chapter 20
The rewards of deceit
(David)

From the balcony of his office David stared out over the city of Jerusalem as he had done a hundred times before, except this time it felt different. Instead of hope, or pride, or gratitude to God, all he felt was relief. He had carried the guilt of his adultery for almost a month now and the burden of it had become almost too much. He could not sleep, every report or update he received was filled with concern or doubt, even the good news seemed to contain threats and concerns instead of moments to rejoice.

He tried not to think of the fifty men who had died with Uriah. He had never envisioned that to be part of the plan. All he needed, wanted, was for Uriah to 'removed.' *Removed*, David realized that he could not even say the word 'killed' in his thoughts, but that is truly what it was. Success left a terrible taste in his heart. He shook his head and forced the thoughts from his mind and heart, thinking instead of the future. Bathsheba.

She had been on his mind from the moment he saw her. From lust, to regret, to fear, to deceit, to murder. The last word came to mind before he could stop it, but he quickly corrected those thoughts and justified it. The damage caused by a king's adulterous relationship with her would have been too great for the people to bear. David felt confident that even his advisors would have agreed, if had he chosen to consult them. Joab's participation in the plan showed him how important it was to keep this all hidden. It was unfortunate, but David believed that even God understood the reasoning and his actions. He believed Bathsheba would also be in support of what had to be done.

David knew that without the support of Uriah, Bathsheba would be destitute and alone. Except for her servant, the one who had twice glared at him for his actions. Once after the night he had laid with Bathsheba and then when she came to deliver the message that Bathsheba was pregnant with his child. What was her name? David wondered if she could also be a threat down the line, then shook his head. He was not concerned, knowing that he needed to put the next part of the plan in motion, now that Uriah was gone.

David felt the idea of marrying Bathsheba immediately after the week of mourning would not only show the people the deep love and respect he had for Uriah, it would allow him to shield the fact that she was pregnant with his child and if necessary, have the midwives claim it was an early birth. David was confident that Bathsheba would appreciate the gesture and protection of her reputation, he would avoid being destitute and alone while raising a child. She was a beautiful women and David was confident that he could fall in love with more than her beauty once she was his wife.

David smiled and took a deep breath as he looked out over the city again. Despite all the challenges and shifting of strategies, his plan had finally worked out for the best of all involved.

David heard his assistant clear his throat behind him and turned to see him standing there with a stack of parchment in his hands. "Nathan has given me the names of the men and their families who were under Uriah's command. He is waiting downstairs to deliver the letters once they have been written," the assistant said. David was surprised how fast Nathan had acted to produce the list. David was planning to write the letters later in the day, but with Nathan waiting downstairs, he decided to write them now.

"Set them on my desk and tell Nathan I will get them to him as soon as they are completed," David replied curtly and dismissed his assistant with a motion of his hand. David thought of Nathan and how bothersome he had been the past month. Did he know? David suddenly remembered how he had seen him coming from Bathsheba's residence following Uriah's last visit. Had Bathsheba confided in him during that visit? Had her servant told him about what had happened? If so, why had he remained silent and what was he planning?

The fear and shame of such a discovery flooded back into his mind, then the thought of the consequences of it. He asked to personally deliver the letter to Bathsheba, instead of David doing it. Was there more behind Nathan's request than he expressed, David wondered, and his mind started racing again. He hated how, despite his best efforts, this one moment of weakness kept coming back to haunt him. How far was he willing to go to make it all go away forever?

David finally managed to get his thoughts and fears back under control. *Nathan knew nothing*, he finally decided and walked to his desk. Next to the stack of parchment was a list of the names of Uriah's men and under each name, were one or more additional family member names. David sat down and picked up the list and began reading each name on the list. Memories of some of the men came rushing through his mind, whether in battle or sitting around a fire late at night with them. The names began to take on flesh and become more than just letters on a piece of parchment. For the first time he had clarity regarding what the consequences of his sin looked like on others, not just on himself. Even understanding how his ongoing attempt at keeping it hidden had increased the consequences, not reduced or eliminated them.

His heart grew heavier with each new name that he read, almost melting in his chest as he thought about the loss and impact the deaths of these men would mean to their families, all because of his lust and sin. Instead of losing the respect of one man by confessing his sin to him, his ongoing efforts to hide it had cost the lives of over 50 men. How much further would he allow this to go before his conscience would say 'enough,' he wondered? Then just as suddenly, the feelings of guilt stopped as he read the last two names: Bathsheba, and Talia her servant.

Somehow, after reading Bathsheba's name, the guilt and shame was quickly replaced with the renewed understanding that protecting her honor and the honor of kingdom was worth as many lives as needed. As he started writing the letters, David was confident that God understood this as well. He knew the one he would write to Bathsheba would be far different from the ones to families of Uriah's men. That one would be sealed and for her eyes only.

Chapter 21
The rewards of deceit
(Nathan)

It was late evening when Nathan was finally able to climb into his bed after one of the longest and most difficult days of his life. All the memories of the day came rushing back into his mind as if salt were being poured onto an open wound in his heart. So many tears, so much hurt, eruptions of anger and bitterness, but mostly disbelief that their son, father, spouse or friend was gone. As the messenger, Nathan felt every emotion from them pour over and through him.

As he laid there, he tried sifting through the various memories and ways he could help comfort each family. Then the memory of Bathsheba's response seemed to stay with him, as if beckoning him to learn from it. Once again, Bathsheba's response had been far different from the other families, just like the first time he delivered Uriah's message to her. Although he knew the messages were far different from the first time, for the most part there was a commonality of feelings among the families. With Bathsheba, no matter how hard he tried, he could not seem to grasp what she was truly feeling.

As she broke the seal and read David's letter, Nathan saw that HER early responses were typical in nature, but they somehow turned darker and deeper as she continued reading. When she had finished reading, she looked up and almost glared at Nathan. Just as he was saying "I'm so sorry for your..." she suddenly excused herself from his presence, not even allowing him to finish his condolence statement to her.

Where the other families wanted to ask questions, somehow trying to understand the how and why of the news, she had simply stormed off in tears, leaving him alone with Talia, her servant. As before, Talia motioned toward the door as she ran up the stairs after her employer, which Nathan understood was a signal to let himself out again.

He tossed and turned in his bed all night thinking about it. Was it an overflow of anger from the wife of a warrior who knew this letter would someday come? Anger toward the king who had recruited and sent her husband off to war so many years ago, leaving her alone? Or was it just anger at him for being the bearer of bad news? Whatever words David had chosen to use to console her in his letter, they had failed miserably. As exhausted and emotionally drained as he was, it was nearly morning before he finally drifted off to sleep.

The following day, Nathan learned that David had called for a special week of mourning for all of Jerusalem following the news of the death of Uriah and his men. This generated an outpouring of gifts and condolences being sent to the families to help encourage them during this time of mourning.

Nathan took the time to visit each family member again, to offer his counsel and prayers for them. The only place he was not invited in to speak in person was at Bathsheba's. Talia simply said she was not entertaining visitors at this time, thanked him, and shut the door. Nathan's heart was heavy knowing that all the other families were surrounded by friends and family to help them through this difficult time, but the only friend Bathsheba had was Talia.

At the end of the week of mourning, Nathan was deeply surprised and disturbed by news he overheard from a merchant during his visit to the market area. When he first heard it, he shook his head and assumed it was just gossip, but then it was confirmed by several others and even an official of the palace that Nathan recognized in the market. Apparently, David had announced that in honor of the commitment by Uriah and David's commitment to protect and support Bathsheba should this ever happen, David had married

Bathsheba.[1] Nathan was shocked, not by the news of the marriage, which made Bathsheba David's fourth wife, but by the fact that David had never asked for his counsel on the matter during the past week.

Nathan found himself almost running to the palace to confirm what he had heard. David's assistant did confirm the news when Nathan arrived. He was also informed that David's schedule was so filled with new husband duties that he would not be able to meet with Nathan today, but he would try to make time tomorrow. He would send a messenger when his schedule was clear, essentially dismissing Nathan.

Nathan once again found himself standing outside the entrance of the palace, trying to comprehend all that had happened and was happening around him. Although on the surface there was even a sense of wisdom behind David's decision, something was wrong. He glanced over at Bathsheba's nearby residence. Would Talia be there or was she now living in the palace with Bathsheba? Out of concern, he knocked several times on the door, but no one answered. *That was a fast transition*, he thought. This discussion and decision to marry had to have taken place several days before today. Nathan realized that this decision had not even waited until after the week of mourning. *Why the rush?* Nathan wondered as he slowly walked back to the temple.

Nathan was not sure if the doubt he was feeling was simply out of hurt pride for David not consulting him on the matter, or because he learned the news from someone other than David. The more he thought about it, the more he felt like it was a righteous anger. Kings and those after God's own heart had always consulted their advisors on such important spiritual matters. Why hadn't David?

Nathan spent the rest of the day in deep prayer and fasting as he sorted through and tried to piece together the various dreams God had given him the past month. He pleaded with God to reveal their meaning and purpose, but God remained silent to his requests. That silence from God would last for another eight months.

For the most part David had also remained silent during those eight months. There were brief interactions that Nathan had with David, but nothing close to what it had been before the loss of Uriah and David's marriage to Bathsheba. Nathan tried to understand why or what had changed their close relationship and made it so distant. He thought of his prior interactions with Bathsheba and wondered if it was perhaps her influence and apparent dislike of him that had changed David's heart toward him? No matter what it was, Nathan could not find the reason or the remedy to restore it.

Although God and David were silent, a great deal happened in those eight months. Soon after their marriage, David announced that Bathsheba was with child and there was rejoicing in the city. And although earlier than expected, last night it was announced that Bathsheba had delivered a son to David. God also chose later that evening to end his silence with Nathan, sending him a dream that broke his heart and shook his faith.[2]

Nathan sat in his bed, his heart and mind racing at the clarity and meaning of the dream and the message God had given him to share with David. How could he have missed it. Nathan wondered as he thought through the various dreams and experiences he had since his first dreams about David had started nine months ago. Having the truth now revealed in the dream, he slowly began putting all the pieces together.

All the events, concerned feelings and observations he had during the time finally made sense, however he did not understand why God had allowed it to continue? Why not stop it on the first night with Bathsheba, or before it even happened? Why hadn't God sent him a revealing dream about David and what he was about to do the first night before lying with Bathsheba, instead of sending him a dream about David standing at a dangerous crossroad? Or a dream that would reveal his plans to have Uriah killed, instead of sending him a dream of him trapped on a tower, watching from a distance as David decided whether to take the easy path of deceit that led to his ruin, or the hard path of confession and the short-term consequences that would ultimately lead to his redemption and peace? Why had he not forced Joab to refuse David's orders and spare Uriah and his men? Why had he not moved Uriah's heart to reject Joab's plan as the other leaders had? Or why hadn't Bathsheba just confided in him as to what happened the first time they had met, so that he could have confronted David immediately and prevented all of this from ever happening? Nathan even struggled trying to understand why he personally had not pressed David further with questions and given him more opportunities to be open about what had happened?

Late into the night Nathan thought about the hundred different opportunities that every person involved along the way could have had to possibly change the path that David had followed. But it seemed each person took the path of least resistance, whether from fear, shame, pride or laziness.

It was close to daybreak when God finally revealed the answer by reminding Nathan of the times he sat and watched the cases being brought before David for ruling. Each of those cases not only told a story of *free will,* where people either chose to do the right thing or the wrong thing before God. It also told a story of whether a person would choose to stand against such abuse, to accept it, or worse, to go along with it. How the greater the power one held over the other, the greater the potential for abuse and damage. Nathan now realized that even a man after God's own heart was not immune to such thoughts or actions. Just like David made his ruling over the cases brought before him, God allowed David to choose what story he would embrace. Instead of trying to resolve and settle the matter himself in a righteous way as king, his choice would ultimately force God, the only power greater than him, to be the judge in the matter.

Nathan knew that it is a fearful and terrifying thing to fall into the hands of the living God. The ruling would be made, and the consequences dealt out accordingly. David had not only chosen to abuse his power and position to sleep with Bathsheba for his own desires, but he also then continued to use it to cover his growing list of sins tied to it.

Nathan's heart sank knowing that the pain and suffering would not only continue for those impacted by David sin, but his sin would have catastrophic implications on the future of his family as well. *A death of innocence* was the best way that Nathan could describe the impact of David's sin. It had stolen the innocence of a wife. It had killed the innocent lives of a loyal friend and fifty innocent soldiers. It had shattered the reputation of a trusted general who chose to be an accomplice with David instead of opposing it. It had forever tarnished his legacy and trust with the people of Israel and with the loyalty of his soldiers and leaders. And more importantly, God had revealed to Nathan that his sin would cost David the life of an innocent child, his newborn son.

Nathan tried to understand God's purpose in taking the life of a child who did nothing wrong. Was it to protect the child from the shame and abuse that Nathan knew society would inflict on him, as if he was somehow the reason for David's sin and why so many would end up suffering from it? Was it a sacrificial atonement for David's sin? Was it a warning and example to current and future leaders of the dangerous consequences should they chose to abuse their position of God-given authority? Was it a foreshadowing of a future event or sacrifice that God was currently keeping silent about? Perhaps it could be some or all the above reasons, but it was not for Nathan to disagree or to cast judgement on God's will. God had a purpose for everything.

As the morning sun chased away the darkness and he prepared to visit David to deliver God's word and judgement, Nathan grasped something that had never crossed his mind before. To protect the truth of the baby and his sin from being discovered or made known, David was even willing to embrace and justify the need for the murder of prominent individuals, even friends. Was Nathan's life any different or more valuable in David's eyes than Uriah's? How far was David willing to go to protect his lie? How far was Nathan willing to go to reveal the truth?

Nathan wondered how many people in this generation, even past generations, had found themselves in the same 'moment of truth' situation. Being forced to either remain silent and preserve their life, or to speak up and risk their life for the truth? He then wondered how many people, with far less than their lives at risk who, although had within their power to protect the innocent by revealing the truth, instead chose to allow a lie to exist or continue. Was their silence about the sin any less guilty than the sin committed by their leader? It was the way of the coward who feared man more than they feared God.

He felt strengthened, even shook off the fear, when he remembered that it all depended upon whose glory you sought or protected in the situation, your own, or God's. David might kill him, that could even be part of God's plan, but Nathan knew that protecting God's glory and honor mattered far more to him than protecting David's. He could not imagine what his life would be like, carrying the guilt and shame of hiding or protecting some person's sin, even one as powerful and great as David, all because he was afraid of the personal consequences of revealing it.

Even the idea of choosing to measure the weight of someone's sin, somehow setting a limit as to where you would draw the line if a person crossed it before confronting them on it seemed to Nathan to be complicit in the outcome. Worse yet, was even adjusting that line according to the person, or their position. Nathan knew that both were simply acts of a coward hidden behind sinful justification. Although he knew that God was filled with mercy, he also knew he did not bless cowards or liars.

As a man of God who sought only His glory, Nathan would not be a coward today, or ever. He then paused at the thought of the last word. Nathan knew that David had once professed and held to that same line of conviction, yet then chose to cross it. What situation in his life could occur that would find him so spiritually weak that he would even consider having a change of heart? Would he even recognize the moment, or would that realization come only after he had already given in to the fear and cowardice of it? All he knew was that today was not going to be that day.

As Nathan walked with a heavy heart toward the palace for what could be the last meeting he would ever have with David, he realized that how David responded to God's message would determine everything. David's humility and repentance would reopen the door to God's grace and mercy, or he could take the road of pride and selfishness that would take him even further down the path of darkness that he had chosen up to this point. Although Nathan hoped David would choose wisely, he knew that his responsibility was to obey and trust in God.

[1] 2 Samuel 11:26-27
[2] 2 Samuel 12:1-14

Chapter 22
A house of lies.
(David)

As he held his newborn son in his arms, tears now streaming down his own face, David suddenly realized that he was standing on the same balcony, even in the same place, that he had been standing that fateful day 9 months ago. The day that he had turned from the counsel of God and instead followed the passion and counsel of his flesh.

Although he felt crushed, embarrassed and his heart broken into a thousand pieces from Nathan's message from God, he somehow felt relieved that the house of lies he had created to cover his sin had finally been revealed and destroyed. Board by board, brick by brick, he had been building this decrepit house of lies. From the first crumbling cornerstone he had laid on the crooked foundation of the lie and manipulation of Bathsheba, to each piece of rotted wood and crumbling stone of lies and sins he used to cover that lie, David knew the house would eventually collapse upon the weight of the very materials it was made from. Yet from the darkest counsel, he allowed himself to be convinced that just one more board or brick, paid for by just one more piece of his soul and spirit, was all that would be needed to prevent its collapse. He knew it was a lie, that building a life, or dream, or passion on any foundation other than God would fail. Yet he kept building and kept paying the inner costs for it.

David felt spiritually bankrupt and emotionally exhausted, yet relieved that he no longer had to keep feeding the insatiable beast his sin had created. He could finally lay down the bent and crooked tools he had been using and finally rest again. The personal and spiritual cost of the house of lies was higher than he could ever have imagined paying from his own dark counsel. He glanced down at the innocent child he held in his arms and tears once again began to flow down his face and then his body began to shake again as he failed to hold back his sorrow.

Once he had regained control of his broken emotions, David began to think through the message Nathan had delivered to him from God. Had he missed something in the message? Was there a way to save his child from the consequences of his sin? David no longer cared about what would happen to himself, in fact he was resigned to the idea that he would be dragged outside and stoned by his own people or killed by his soldiers once the truth was revealed. He almost longed for such an ending if it was God's will but was hoping to find a different ending for the innocent child he held in his arms.

David remembered that he had tried to dismiss Nathan three times when he had been informed of his arrival and the urgent need to meet with the King. With each dismissal, Nathan made it clearer that he would not be leaving until he met with the king. He remembered that he had buried his sin so deeply and had justified his actions so thoroughly that he had no idea what Nathan could want with him. He was expecting urgent news, but instead Nathan presented him with a disturbing case between two parties. He was surprised that Nathan seemed uncomfortable as he began laying out the details of the case to him.

"There were two men in a certain town, one rich and the other poor. The rich man had a very large number of sheep and cattle, but the poor man had nothing except one little ewe lamb he had bought. He raised it, and it grew up with him and his children. It shared his food, drank from his cup and even slept in his arms. It was like a daughter to him. Now a traveler came to the rich man, but the rich man refrained from taking one of his own sheep or cattle to prepare a meal for the traveler who had come to him. Instead, he took the ewe lamb that belonged to the poor man and prepared it for the one who had come to him." Nathan had finished the story and then had looked up to see how David would respond.

Although the case Nathan presented to him was simple, the idea of someone abusing their power and position to take advantage of one so innocent and vulnerable burned inside of him in such a manner that David burned with anger at the man and his actions. He remembered standing from his chair and almost shouting his judgement back at Nathan. "As surely as the LORD lives, the man who did this must die! He must pay for that lamb four times over, because he did such a thing and had no pity."

Instead of nodding and agreeing with his passing of judgement on the man, Nathan only stared back at David, as if waiting for him to realize the truth behind the story. Seeing that David had missed it, Nathan took a step toward David and then looked into his eyes as if trying to find something hidden in his soul.

"You are the man! This is what the LORD, the God of Israel, says: 'I anointed you king over Israel, and I delivered you from the hand of Saul. I gave your master's house to you, and your master's wives into your arms. I gave you all Israel and Judah. And if all this had been too little, I would have given you even more. Why did you despise the word of the LORD by doing what is evil in his eyes? You struck down Uriah the Hittite with the sword and took his wife to be your own. You killed him with the sword of the Ammonites. Now, therefore, the sword will never depart from your house, because you despised me and took the wife of Uriah the Hittite to be your own." Nathan said sternly and clearly to him, the nervousness gone from his voice as if God himself was speaking the words.

David remembered stepping back and almost falling into his chair, thinking 'how could he have known?' and then realized the judgement he had pronounced on the man. He had called for his death for such crimes and now that same judgement would come upon him from God. He was jarred back to the moment as Nathan's voice, with the same power and authority of God, continued the message from God.

"This is what the LORD says: 'Out of your own household I am going to bring calamity on you. Before your very eyes I will take your wives and give them to one who is close to you, and he will sleep with your wives in broad daylight. You did it in secret, but I will do this thing in broad daylight before all Israel.'"

That was when David finally realized when the cornerstone of his house of lies had begun. When he was more worried about keeping it secret than confessing it and bringing it to God. "I have sinned against the LORD." David stated and bowed his head as if waiting to be struck down by the hand of God as he sat in his chair.

Nathan replied, "The LORD has taken away your sin. You are not going to die. But because by doing this you have shown utter contempt for the LORD, the son born to you will die." When Nathan had finished proclaiming God's judgement, he waited as if waiting to answer David's questions, but he had remained silent in his grief and shame. As if understanding the reason for David's silence, Nathan quietly left the room.

As he sat there, he did not give pause or even try to understand the list of consequences from his sin that Nathan had pronounced from God. The only thing he could think of was the judgement God had placed upon his son for his sins. He shook off the tears and called for one of his servants to bring him his son. Would he be able to hold him one more time before God took him home to be with him?

His mind raced back to the present and as he held the little child in his arms. David thanked God for the bittersweet blessing of seeing his son one more time. As he looked at the child's face, he thought about the future consequences that God had declared on him and his family, he then envied the idea of its death and the ability to miss such tragedy and turmoil. Suddenly, the baby began the concerning cough again and began crying between its gasps for breath.

David called out to one of the child's attendants, who then took the child and carried him back to his mother. As the child disappeared beyond the door, he thought about Bathsheba and what he had done to her honor, her husband, and now her firstborn. He thought about Uriah and how he abused his trust and not only took away his future, but his most precious blessing from God. He thought about Uriah's men and their families, how he taken away their fathers, sons, husbands, and how their family's lives would be far more difficult without them.

"Why oh God, have you taken away my sin and spared my life? I had pronounced judgement on the rich man in the story for far smaller of a sin than mine, so why spare me?" David cried out and fell on his knees. "Please take my life instead and spare the life of my child," he pleaded. Somehow by God's judgement, David knew that God was not done with him. That he had more in store for him than a life of shame and regret. He knew that he had broken something so precious and valuable that even though mended, his relationship with God was somehow less than what it had been before.

David knew that God preferred a humble and contrite heart over sacrifice and offerings, so he decided that was the path he would do his best to take from here forward. He knew it would be difficult and filled with danger and risk, but it was arriving at the desired destination that mattered more than the journey itself. He had spent the past nine months trying to hide something that ended up costing the lives of many innocent people. As the anointed of God, if the truth of that sin remained hidden, it could bring God's name and honor into that sin. To protect that honor, he decided he would reveal and announce what was hidden and no longer worry about the consequences or shame of his sin that others may inflict on him.

He sat down at his desk and started to write a letter, a letter that would be copied and then delivered and announced across the kingdom.

Chapter 23
An accomplice to sin
(Joab)

"I was following orders!" Joab almost yelled back at the group of red-faced and angry men standing around him. He was livid at David. He knew he could have avoided or controlled the chaos of the moment if David had sent a single letter to him, instead of a letter to each of the leaders detailing his sin with Bathsheba, his involvement in the deceit and eventual death of Uriah and his men, and how he had sinned against God. Now Joab was in a fight for his life with the men he commanded.

"You could have refused or asked why! Instead, you blindly embraced it and even developed the very plan that led to Uriah's and his men's death!" Another stepped forward and shouted over the grumbling.

"No, that was David's idea, not mine," Joab tried to defend himself, he thought. *Instead of confessing his sin, why didn't David simply change the narrative?* They could have just as easily created a back story of why Uriah's death was best, even plant seeds of doubt that would undermine Uriah's character. Instead, David wrote an apology letter to the families of those affected by his sin, a letter that was to be read to all the people of Israel who had trusted in his leadership and his protection, and an apology to God for any damage his sin had caused to their faith and their trust in their Creator and His anointed king. He ended the letter by asking for their forgiveness.

"I doubt that!" another yelled and stepped forward as if wanting to close with Joab, but Abishai stepped in front of him and made it clear to him and the others is that the only way anyone would harm his brother was going through him first.

"Joab's right! It was David's plan," Amos said and stepped forward and to the side of Abishai. "I saw David's reaction the moment I reported Uriah's death to him. He was relieved, not angry. Joab was only following the kings' orders!" Amos yelled over the growing clamor of disgruntled voices and continued to stand next to Abishai. Joab was relieved to see that his training and investment in Amos's loyalty was paying off so quickly.

"He still could have stopped it," the man growled angrily and looked past the two soldiers and directly at Joab. Joab tried to find a way to quickly change the narrative from blaming him to something else. The idea worked once before on Amos, perhaps it would work again with others.

"You're right!" Joab yelled and held up his hand and waited for the men to calm down enough to allow him to speak. "You're right," he said again, except softer and then acted as if he was waiting for silence to say more. The admission of guilt seemed to catch the group off guard and eventually they lowered their voices as if hoping Joab would continue down the path of ownership of his part in the death of Uriah and his men. "I could have. I should have asked the reason for such a treacherous and deceitful plan from the King. Now to my shame and eternal guilt, knowing the truth behind such orders, I will carry that decision and the death of those men to my grave," he said and paused for effect; he then pushed past Abishai and Amos, and stepped amongst the men who moments ago were trying to get to him.

"Now that I know the truth, and the part that I unknowingly played in it, I do deserve death. I would even feel better knowing that those memories will no longer haunt me from this day forward. Whoever feels they need to be my executioner, step forward and drive your sword through my heart!" he yelled, then closed his eyes and spread his arms wide. To say he was relieved that no one stepped forward to honor his fake request for swift judgement would be an understatement. Joab knew it was a gamble but felt confident that others would not be as quick and willing to act on such an opportunity as he was toward Uriah. Joab slowly lowered his arms and then his head and walked back behind the protection of his brother and Amos.

"Brothers, we need to find a way to move forward from here. I need your counsel…" Joab began but was interrupted.

"Don't claim to be my brother or offer your professed desire to hear my valued counsel," a man said and glared at Joab. "You forget that was your desire and claim the last time we met, all the while knowing the truth and then lying to us. At least David owned his sin," the man said angrily.

Then another stepped forward and continued the renewed attack. "Do you really believe your false humility and veiled lies will somehow remove your guilt, or regain our trust in you ever again? The only reason you still live is because we chose to extend mercy to you, the same mercy you chose not to extend to Uriah and his men. However, do not misinterpret this extended mercy from us or the consequences of it. Because you were a willing accomplice to their deaths," the man paused, then shook his head before continuing. "No, we will now question every order you give, doubt every motive you profess to have, and withhold any honor to whatever victory you bring as our general. We will give you only what is required of our position, and no more. Although we might follow you out of duty, we will look forward to the day when another takes your place," he said glaring and then turned and walked out of the meeting area. Moments later, one, then eventually all of them nodded their confirmation of what the man had said and left.

Joab, Abishai and Amos stood in silence as the last of the men filed out of the tent. Although he was relieved that the meeting had not ended in his death, he knew that his years of careful plotting and positioning that had allowed him to become the second most powerful man in Israel had unraveled before his eyes in a moment. Where moments before David's letter arrived, he thought the knowledge and truth of David's orders to have Uriah killed had been a sweet blessing, a blessing that would have given him the most powerful leverage tool with which to manipulate and control David. That tool was now not only lost, but had turned into a bitter poison that David had caused him to drink as well.

He looked around the nearly empty tent and could even see the doubt on the faces of his brother and Amos and the anger continued to grow inside of him. Before the letter arrived, should there ever have been a need to overthrow the leadership and direct the kingdom such as now, he would have had an army that would have supported him, even fought to place him in power. Now the only power he held was the loyalty and trust of these two men.

Joab knew it would take years to rebuild the power and influence he had before David's letter arrived. Perhaps it would never be reclaimed under David's rule, assuming the people would allow him to continue to rule them. He looked down at the letter David had written sitting on his desk and decided it was a stupid ill-advised letter from a weak and sinful leader. He knew if he was to ever regain the lost power and position, it would only come through someone else. Just as his men had made clear to him, he would support David's wishes and orders out of duty, but he would be ever alert and watchful for any opportunity that may arise.

Chapter 24
A history of the king
(Nathan)

With his cloak wrapped tightly around his aging body for warmth, Nathan waited on the palace veranda for King Solomon to arrive for their scheduled meeting. Nathan held the railing for added support and balance as he glanced out over the city and smiled at the many memories of incidents that occurred here. It was king David's favorite place to pray and meditate during his 33 years ruling from Jerusalem. It was also the birthplace of his greatest sin and the many heartbreaks that followed.

David had confided in him that he once considered either tearing down the balcony or bricking over the doorway to it because of those memories, but had then he realized the power behind those memories. He had even come to treasure those memories and use them as a reminder of the evil he was capable of without God. The very same place that he had cried out to God for wisdom and strength was where he had turned away from that strength and power for his own selfish gain.

"It keeps me humble," David had said to him with a smile during one of the countless times he had sought Nathan's counsel following his repentance of his relationship with Bathsheba and his murder of Uriah and his men almost 30 years ago.

Nathan took a deep breath of the cool autumn air and thought back to the days following David's letter to the people. Most people who confess their sins whisper it to a priest or quietly to the people they had sinned against. Not David. Nathan smiled at the memory. He wrote a letter detailing his sin and had it copied and read to everyone who would listen. It was an uncommon act of humility and surrender that once again showed that he was a man after God's own heart.

There was no deceitful strategy or sinister motive behind the writing of the letter, as if trying to win the hearts of the people. Although he knew that God had forgiven him, David expected the people of Israel to stone him once they read the letter. But he did not care about them or what they would do; he cared only about being right with God.

Not only did that act of humility and honesty save him from death at the hands of the people, it granted him the forgiveness he never expected to receive from them and the continued love and trust in him that he felt he did not deserve.

Although God continued to bless his efforts during his time as king and protector of Israel, he did not withhold the judgments that he declared and foretold regarding the consequences of David's sin.

Despite David's 7 days of constant prayer and fasting, crying out to God to spare his son's life, God took the child. Nathan remembered David asking him if God had allowed the child to live during those seven days so that David could understand the grief and sorrow the families of Uriah's men experienced during their seven days of mourning. Nathan remembered being surprised by the question and realization of the timeline. He had shrugged and told David that God's ways and purposes are always higher than ours.

God had also not withheld the calamity that he foretold about David's family. How much of the calamity had been a by-product of David's sin Nathan did not know exactly. He did know that sin was a yeast that once planted by the past example and justification of another, can slowly expand into the various aspects of not only the members of his own family, but an entire kingdom as well. Nathan's heart grew heavy at the thought of how it had worked its way through David's family during the remainder of his life as king.

One of his sons had slept with his sister out of his own lust and selfish pursuit.[1] One of his sons plotted and eventually killed his brother[2], then after being forgiven, turned and plotted to overthrow his father[3]. Then, the once trusted men from his armies and the men that followed them joined that son in rebellion[4]. To launch the rebellion, the son slept with David's concubines in broad daylight for all to see, and then lead the army to seek out and kill his own father, all for power. Even the smallest amount of yeast allowed into a life can eventually expand through the whole batch in time.

That same dangerous yeast did not spare those who had chosen to be an accomplice to sin, or even those who, out of fear, did not speak up against it. Joab's selfish pursuit of power, position, and respect eventually caught up with him. The very thing he wanted most was slowly and methodically taken from him over time. The people whom he had manipulated and taken advantage of turned on him. Even his own brother chose David over him. It was King Solomon that had Joab put to death as one of the last requests of his father David.[5]

Nathan also knew that even the innocent was not immune to the infection of the yeast of sin as he thought about Bathsheba, the death of Uriah and his men, and of the first son Bathsheba had born him. Sin knows no barriers. Nathan shook off the darker memories and tried to refocus his mind on more righteous thoughts.

Despite the apparent darkness in the last part of David's life, there was so much light that God displayed through him, light that would also be passed on to some of his family as well. The city of Rabbah was eventually captured, the nation of Israel was established and secured, and the seemingly unending wars to protect it had ended under his rule. David also had another son with Bathsheba. A son that God had blessed with such wisdom that Nathan was confident his kingly leadership would provide an endless potential for good if he chose to follow in his father's footsteps in being a man after God's own heart.

"Nathan! It is good to see you my friend," King Solomon almost shouted as he stepped out onto the veranda to join him. "Sorry if I have kept you waiting."

"Not at all my king. I was just cherishing the many memories I had of your father and the many hours we shared on this balcony, and in life," Nathan replied with a smile as he turned and embraced the King. "He was a remarkable man, and I will miss him dearly now that he is gone," Nathan replied, and Solomon nodded and smiled.

"Yes, he was, and I will miss him too," Solomon said softly at first then suddenly his demeanor lightened, and he smiled. "Did I ever share with you a letter he gave to me before his passing?" he asked Nathan, who shook his head. "It has become my most treasured source of wisdom and direction. I have even memorized every word of it and refer to it often," Solomon stated and then seemed to gather his thoughts as he took Nathan by the arm and walked with him back to the railing of the balcony. As they looked out over the city of Jerusalem before them, he began to recite from memory the treasured words of a father to his beloved son.

> *My son, do not forget my teaching, but keep my commands in your heart, for they will prolong your life many years and bring you peace and prosperity. Let love and faithfulness never leave you; bind them around your neck, write them on the tablet of your heart. Then you will win favor and a good name in the sight of God and man.*

Trust in the LORD with all your heart and lean not on your own understanding; in all your ways submit to him, and he will make your paths straight. Do not be wise in your own eyes; fear the LORD and shun evil. This will bring health to your body and nourishment to your bones.

Honor the LORD with your wealth, with the first fruits of all your crops; then your barns will be filled to overflowing, and your vats will brim over with new wine. My son, do not despise the LORD's discipline, and do not resent his rebuke, because the LORD disciplines those he loves, as a father the son he delights in.

Blessed are those who find wisdom, those who gain understanding, for she is more profitable than silver and yields better returns than gold. She is more precious than rubies; nothing you desire can compare with her. Long life is in her right hand; in her left hand are riches and honor. Her ways are pleasant ways, and all her paths are peace. She is a tree of life to those who take hold of her; those who hold her fast will be blessed.

By wisdom the LORD laid the earth's foundations, by understanding he set the heavens in place; by his knowledge the watery depths were divided, and the clouds let drop the dew. My son, do not let wisdom and understanding out of your sight, preserve sound judgment and discretion; they will be life for you, an ornament to grace your neck. Then you will go on your way in safety, and your foot will not stumble. When you lie down, you will not be afraid; when you lie down, your sleep will be sweet.

Have no fear of sudden disaster or of the ruin that overtakes the wicked, for the LORD will be at your side and will keep your foot from being snared. Do not withhold good from those to whom it is due, when it is in your power to act. Do not say to your neighbor, "Come back tomorrow and I'll give it to you"—when you already have it with you.

Do not plot harm against your neighbor, who lives trustfully near you. Do not accuse anyone for no reason—when they have done you no harm. Do not envy the violent or choose any of their ways. For the LORD detests the perverse but takes the upright into his confidence. The LORD's curse is on the house of the wicked, but he blesses the home of the righteous. He mocks proud mockers but shows favor to the humble and oppressed. The wise inherit honor, but fools get only shame.

As he listened to Solomon and the words David had shared with him[6], Nathan knew without a shadow of doubt that David not only understood the damage of his sin, but he also learned from every aspect of it and had repented of it. More importantly, David also knew the only source of true value and peace in life came from God. He smiled at the revelation God had shared with him about David, that the messiah and savior of the world would be born from his lineage.

From his youth to his death, and despite a moment of darkness in the middle, David had been a man after God's own heart.

---

[1] 2 Samuel 13: all
[2] 2 Samuel 14: all
[3] 2 Samuel 15: all
[4] 2 Samuel 16-17: all
[5] 1 Kings 2:31-35
[6] Proverbs 3: all

Chapter 25
Life reflections
(author's notes)

Since that life changing day when my wife and I made Jesus Lord in 1991, we have had the incredible joy and blessing of being a part of many ministries and church plantings for the glory of God. Although we were excited, and trusting, as dripping wet Christians stepping out of the waters of baptism and into a part of God's earthly kingdom, we also brought with us years of non-kingdom business experiences and understandings. A worldly wisdom that was not naïve to the potential for evil that is often waiting within the hearts of humankind. An evil that is waiting for not only those in positions of power and leadership, but also for those who are witness to it, or affected by it. Individuals who could have stopped it (great or small), but out of selfish ambition or cowardice (fear) did nothing, or worse, became an accomplice to it.

I wish we could tell you that this potential for evil and abuse in leadership (or being an accomplice to it) only occurred in large churches, or that it only happens to young men and women placed in positions of authority before they are spiritually ready. Unfortunately, that would not reflect our personal experiences or even church history throughout time (Old Testament, New Testament and from the 1st Century until today).

None of us, including my wife and I, are above such potential for evil. What we often forget is that just as we desire to plant and water the seeds of God's word into the hearts of those looking for an eternal relationship with Jesus, Satan is just as busy and determined to plant his own seeds of evil into those same hearts in order to destroy that desire. He's just waiting for the opportunity to water them and make them grow.

From our experience, such abuse of power does not present itself immediately, but waits patiently for an opportunity to germinate. We often witness a gradual transition from the innocent and trusting Uriah's, who are turned into the selfishly ambitious and complicit Amos's. Where one is doomed and removed if they challenge abusive leadership, the other is groomed to ignore the abuses of those they follow. Once that occurs, it is only a matter of time before the selfishly ambitious and complacent Amos's transition into the Joab accomplices waiting for their turn for power.

Whether the opportunity is small or large, it seems everyone is given the opportunity to wield the abusive power of a David (as a parent, as a coworker in business, as a bible talk leader, or minister). Unfortunately, it is the Nathan's of the world who are in such short supply in God's kingdom and the ones that are most needed by leadership. Unfortunately, they are also the most resented by those who desire to abuse such God given authority and power.

If you feel you are above such temptations, then that is the first sign that the evil seed planted within you has already been watered by Satan and is starting to grow.

Pride goes before destruction, a haughty spirit before a fall.
Proverbs 16:18

Sadly, we've personally watched some of the most innocent hearted and talented, men and women, young and mature, fall prey to a haughty spirit and be destroyed by their own pride. That same pride and haughtiness has claimed the best of us and why the Bible is filled with examples of such falls from innocence. God did not include those endless biblical examples to rub our faces in our failures, but to warn us of our greatest weakness and to be on our guard against it. Not only as leaders, but more importantly, as those who witness it.

We often think the Fall of Man in the Garden of Eden is the same as David's Fall with Bathsheba, but they are not. Although both examples resulted in a fall from the safety and protection of God, Adam and Eve's fall was about the desire for power (to become like God), where David's fall was about the abuse of power (to act like God). One is a selfish and arrogant pride; the other is a false humility wrapped in the guise of authority.

As Christians, we understand that the personal desire to become like God is not something that could ever be obtained, nor could it even pose a threat to God's heavenly rule (even Satan learned that lesson and was cast out). However, the abuse of power, when we act like God, that is a direct threat to God's earthly kingdom and to the people within it. It is something God takes very seriously and why he has set such high standards (and consequences) for anyone leading His people.

Unfortunately, the battle to become like God, and to act like God, is still raging today in both the people of the world and the people of God. From our birth, our desire is to be king and ruler of our own lives. We often even want to be in control of the lives of others if it is to our gain (as children, teens, adults). This desire for personal kingship is often the greatest challenge and cost an individual must face and count if they are to leave the world behind and enter God's kingdom. As a Christian, we are essentially surrendering our desire to be God, even stepping down from our self-made throne, and allowing Jesus to be the King of our lives when we say 'Jesus is Lord' at our baptism.

Although as Christians we may have won the 'who is king' battle against Satan, we can still lose the war to him when we begin to 'act like God' for our own selfish gain. Actions that are often disguised as something that is 'best for the kingdom,' yet are often the very thing that brings further pain and suffering to it. That is why the story of the fall of King David with Bathsheba was so important for God to tell, and why He needed it to be told to all generations and in all its shame and dishonor, not glossed over or hidden from history in his Word.

As much as we might desire it, God does not shield His children from the consequences of our sin during our time on earth (except from the eternal death), but he does forgive us of them. Although David is guilty of a series of horrible sins, just as we are, he is not an eternal villain that has joined the forces of evil with Satan. On the contrary, David's life story and kingship provides us with some of the most incredible examples of what faith, humility, selfless leadership, and what love toward God can look like. Sadly, he is a sinful man who somewhere along his walk with God chose to let go of his humility and in his trust in God.

Although he was 'a man after God's own heart,' David's story is also filled with unfortunate examples of the incredible dangers and consequences of becoming a man or woman after our own heart. Choosing to abuse our positions of power and authority as leaders in God's kingdom (church, family, and business). His story is not just for leaders alone, for it also reveals the dangers of being an accomplice to such abuse (Joab), instead of taking a stand against it (no matter what position you may hold). It reveals the dangers of blindly following the direction of our leaders and ignoring true biblical understanding and authority, or even common sense (Uriah). And finally, it demonstrates what having the courage and confidence in God should look like and how that courage allows us to ignore the fears and consequences we might face from those in positions of power (Nathan). To be willing to approach 'the kings' in our lives and humbly address any potential abuse of such power we might see or discover during their reign and to protect them from themselves and Satan's schemes.

Whether you are an elder, deacon or a non-titled member of a fellowship, it is not only your responsibility to support and protect your leaders as they follow Christ, but more importantly, to protect the fellowship of believers from the leadership should they stop following Jesus. To be alert and aware of the subtle temptations Satan uses for leaders to justify the abuse of such power (small or great) and to be ready to address it, and stop it at the beginning, not ignoring it and allowing it to grow to its full destructive potential.

This threat is nothing new to our generation, but the same playbook Satan has used for every person (even angels) to bend them to his will, the same one he tried to use on Jesus and failed. It starts with the temptation of the flesh (what I need that I feel God is not providing me, but I feel he wants me to have), then it moves to selfish ambition and glory (what I feel I deserve for my hard work and incredible talents), and finally the forcing of God's hand to do your will, not His (the need to act on God's behalf to bend his will toward yours).

Where Jesus resisted every temptation presented by Satan following his baptism and time in the desert, it is those same subtle temptations that have been the downfall of even 'the best' of our leaders. We watch an almost endless cycle of history repeating itself, as humble and blessed beginnings of church leadership who desired to serve God, ends in an abuse of power and selfish rule. A rule that no matter how long or short it lasts, ends up changing the destiny of not only their own lives for the worse, but potentially the lives of so many around them who are caught up in it.

On a more personal level, I want you to pray and take a hard look within yourself to discover where you might find yourself in this story, or perhaps who you relate to in it? What warning bells were going off in your head and heart as you read it? Remember, God gave us the story of David's fall for a reason, I just tried to peel back enough of the layers within it to move those mental thoughts the 12 inches they needed to get them from your head (the what) to your heart (the why). When you do, you can better understand those warning bells, how they apply to your life, and how to courageously address them for God's glory.

If I've succeeded in bringing your heart and your mind together in this story, then the next part is where it can get dangerous if not handled in a Spirit filled way with much prayer and trusted advice. Whether you find yourself as David, Joab, Uriah, Nathan, Bathsheba, or a combination of them, there is a potential for a few, if not a flood of emotions to come pouring out. Some of them, resulting from the sins you have committed, you may have locked tightly away in your mind to avoid thinking about them (shame, guilt, regret), perhaps hoping they will never be remembered or discovered. But unless we confess and renounce those sins, there is no true forgiveness and healing. There will be consequences for those sins, but it is better to enter the Kingdom of God with that sin behind you, than to find yourself stand outside of it gnashing your teeth with it still hidden in your back pocket.

Perhaps you were the one sinned against and those sins committed against you have so hardened your heart and stolen your joy and innocence (anger, bitterness, betrayal) that all you are seeking is revenge. I'm not saying that seeking justice is to be ignored, for God is with you and does not forget (no matter how long it takes). However, in your pursuit of justice while pursuing those destructive and sinful emotions, do not find yourself standing next to your abuser as you look upon the gates of heaven. Be free of them (the sins and the hatred toward your abuser).

So before embracing and acting on any of those dark and Satan inspired emotions, I want you to take a moment to read chapter 5 in the book of Galatians. This one short chapter provides a wealth of wisdom that addresses God's view on such abuse. It teaches us how to overcome Satan's temptations when the opportunity presents itself, how we should respond to such abuse in a Spirit filled way, and what God's deepest desire is for us individually and as a fellowship.

I've included it below (NIV version) and have highlighted a few key verses that I hope will prepare you and soften your heart for whatever may come. Preparing you for how the fellowship may respond to your confession and ownership of such abuse of leadership and/or as an accomplice. It will give you the courage and compassion needed to address such leadership abuse that you have either seen and/or were personally harmed by with courage, grace and forgiveness. Either way, pray that it is for God's glory, not your own glory, and that He will bring back the innocence that was lost.

Galatians 5:(all)

It is for freedom that Christ has set us free. Stand firm, then, and do not let yourselves be burdened again by a yoke of slavery.

² Mark my words! I, Paul, tell you that if you let yourselves be circumcised, Christ will be of no value to you at all. ³ Again I declare to every man who lets himself be circumcised that he is obligated to obey the whole law. ⁴ You who are trying to be justified by the law have been alienated from Christ; you have fallen away from grace. ⁵ For through the Spirit we eagerly await by faith the righteousness for which we hope. ⁶ For in Christ Jesus neither circumcision nor uncircumcision has any value. ***The only thing that counts is faith expressing itself through love.***

⁷ You were running a good race. Who cut in on you to keep you from obeying the truth? *⁸ That kind of persuasion does not come from the one who calls you. ⁹ "A little yeast works through the whole batch of dough." ¹⁰ I am confident in the Lord that you will take no* other view. **The one who is throwing you into confusion, whoever that may be, will have to pay the penalty.** ¹¹ Brothers and sisters, if I am still preaching circumcision, why am I still being persecuted? In that case the offense of the cross has been abolished. ¹² As for those agitators, I wish they would go the whole way and emasculate themselves!

Life by the Spirit

¹³ You, my brothers and sisters, were called to be free. But do not use your freedom to indulge the flesh; rather, serve one another humbly in love. ¹⁴ For the entire law is fulfilled in keeping this one command: "Love your neighbor as yourself." ¹⁵ **If you bite and devour each other, watch out or you will be destroyed by each other.**

¹⁶ **So I say, walk by the Spirit, and you will not gratify the desires of the flesh.** ¹⁷ For the flesh desires what is contrary to the Spirit, and the Spirit what is contrary to the flesh. They are in conflict with each other, so that you are not to do whatever you want. ¹⁸ But if you are led by the Spirit, you are not under the law.

¹⁹ The acts of the flesh are obvious: sexual immorality, impurity and debauchery; ²⁰ idolatry and witchcraft; hatred, discord, jealousy, fits of rage, selfish ambition, dissensions, factions ²¹ and envy; drunkenness, orgies, and the like. I warn you, as I did before, that those who live like this will not inherit the kingdom of God.

²² But the fruit of the Spirit is love, joy, peace, forbearance, kindness, goodness, faithfulness, ²³ gentleness and self-control. Against such things there is no law. ²⁴ Those who belong to Christ Jesus have crucified the flesh with its passions and desires. ²⁵ **Since we live by the Spirit, let us keep in step with the Spirit.** ²⁶ **Let us not become conceited, provoking and envying each other.**

God is calling His people to live a Spirit filled life and purpose that is based on His teachings and leadership example as faith expressing itself through love, not on man-made leadership rules or authority hidden behind selfish ambition, control, or power.

The purpose in writing this story is not to incite rebellion, to encourage you to overthrow your church leadership, to quit your fellowship, or to walk away from your relationship with God (although some of those thoughts have crossed my own sinful mind at times when leadership had truly crossed the line of righteousness). Instead, I hope it creates within you the ongoing desire to have the courage, passion and humility to not only protect the fellowship from such abuse for God's glory, but with God's grace and power, to try to bring the fallen leadership back to the innocence it once had. Not only before it is too late for them, but before the full damage of Satan's schemes can be done to the faith and hearts of the fellowship they oversee. The fellowship needs you and whether like David, the leaders believe it in the moment, they will need you when God brings the consequences of their actions into judgement.

To God be the Glory and let love reign.

Richard Hackett Jr.
www.rhackettjr.com

Other novels from the Author!

The Black Dragons
(Historical Fiction/Adventure)

North Carolina - 1775

Growing up on a tobacco plantation should be a simple life, predictable as the changing seasons, but when unlikely friends become entangled in the politics and shifting loyalties of nations, life is anything but simple. What starts as a plan to protect the families living on one small plantation, captures the attention of world powers vying for control of the American Colonies and the Islands of the Caribbean.

With few options available, untried heroes find themselves caught in a deadly struggle to protect their ideals, their freedoms, and their lives. At every turn their friendship and loyalty to each other and to those brave men they come to lead, is tested. Can the innocent companionship of childhood stand in the face of hatred, prejudice, and war between world powers? Will the ideals that they embody become a testimony to a new world vision for an emerging nation?

The Eyes of the Heart
(Christian Suspense/Thriller)

Life is never what it seems.

From the time he took the job with Allen Brooke Inc., Luke's life had gone from one incredible challenge to the next. In the blink of an eye, they transitioned him from writing training manuals for a new game, to putting his very life on the line for the company. He quickly realized that the product was no game at all, and that it had far more uses and dangers for society than he could have ever imagined, and he was clearly not alone in that understanding.

Secret societies and government intelligence agencies were now looking intently into it, and into anyone who was involved with it. His professional and personal life was suddenly thrust into a deadly battle between two political and religious ideologies that he didn't understand but needed to grasp if he had any chance to stop the religious genocide that one of them had planned.

He would need to use every resource his body could call upon, including the most important one that he had yet to learn how to use… **The Eyes of his Heart.**

Everything
The untold story of the rich young ruler
(Historical Christian Fiction)

"Sell everything," Jesus of Nazareth had told the rich young man who had traveled so far to meet him.

This can't be the Messiah, Addi thought as he walked away from the encounter. *The Messiah would have known he had dedicated his whole life to God, building a deep and powerful financial kingdom right under Pilate and Herod's noses. A secret kingdom that now stood ready to equip and supply the Messiah's army once he stepped forward to claim it as the prophecies of old had foretold. Therefore, he can't be the Messiah.*

Yet Addi could not deny the miracles this Jesus had demonstrated, so God must be with him. The man was fearless and bold when he taught the people, and his message was powerful and amazing. However, it was it was also far different from what the Pharisees and Sadducees were teaching; a new teaching that had not gone unnoticed by them.

"What must I do to inherit eternal life?" Addi shook his head, feeling a little confused. Of all the questions he had wanted to ask the man, that was not one of them. Or was it?

Made in the USA
Monee, IL
16 January 2025